Don't Tie the Knot

A TROUBLESOME WEDDING invitation...

When Lord Hamish Montgomery learns his brother is getting married, he vows to stop the wedding. After all, his brother is a duke and is intended for someone else.

A determined bridesmaid...

Georgiana Butterworth is startled when a handsome Scotsman breaks into her bedroom and brandishes money. Evidently, he's mistaken her for her newly engaged sister, since he is trying to bribe her into not marrying his brother. Georgiana knows one thing: she won't permit this man to ruin her sister's chance for everlasting happiness.

A wedding that mustn't be stopped...

Hamish may be determined to stop the wedding, but Georgiana is intent to make certain the wedding happens, no matter what she has to do to distract him.

Other books in the *Wedding Trouble* series:

Dukes Prefer Bluestockings

The Earl's Christmas Consultant

How to Train a Viscount

A Kiss for the Marquess

A Holiday Proposal

DON'T TIE THE KNOT

Chapter One

MONTGOMERY CASTLE
  Scotland
  May 1816

WHEN THE BUTLER PLACED the day's letters on the silver tray, Lord Hamish Montgomery didn't hesitate to set aside his ruling pen and sort through the mail. He had been tardy once and he'd spent the rest of his life making up for his one-time indulgence in laziness.

No matter how responsible Hamish was now, he could never change the fact he'd entered the world eight minutes too late, by which time his twin brother Callum was already comfortably swaddled and crowned heir to the dukedom.

A scarlet seal Hamish didn't recognize graced the outside of one of the letters, and he unfolded the paper over his drafting board. Most likely one of his brother's creditors was asking for money. Callum seemed determined to make his gaming hall the most luxurious in London, if the bills were anything to go by.

Dear Lord Hamish Montgomery:

Mr. and Mrs. Butterworth of Norfolk happily invite you to share the most joyous occasion of their lives when their daughter, Charlotte Butterworth, is forever joined in matrimony to Callum Montgomery, the Duke of Vernon, at the end of the month at St. George's Church in London.

Hamish blinked.

The letter's brevity did not lessen its impact.

The name *Charlotte Butterworth* appeared entirely different from *Lady Isla McIntyre*, Callum's intended.

God in heaven.

"He's getting married in London," Hamish said, conscious his voice was faint.

"Indeed." The butler's carefully cultivated disinterest was normally reassuring, but Hamish frowned.

"London, *England*." Hamish stressed the last word. "Perhaps there are other Londons."

The butler hesitated, as if valiantly searching for another London. "There is a small settlement by that name in the Province of Upper Canada, my lord. In the 1790s the Lieutenant Governor even proposed it to be the capital of the province, though that plan never went forward. It still remains rather smaller than its English counterpart."

"The English need some variety in the names of their capitals."

"You express the sentiment well, my lord, though I believe there were some strategic advantages for defense that appealed to Sitcoe."

Hamish didn't ask his butler where he'd received the information. Highlanders were always immigrating to Canada.

For a moment, hope bloomed in Hamish's chest.

Canada.

That was certainly a better alternative to the *ton*-replete capital. His lips twitched. Wasn't Canada just a flatter Scotland? Not Hamish's preference, though some people might favor the fact that a misstep in Upper Canada was unlikely to send them hurtling to the bottom of a cliff.

A pained expression appeared on the butler's face. "I am afraid it is unlikely His Grace has chosen precisely *that* London in which to marry. St. George's is a fashionable church for weddings. I believe it is located at Hanover Square."

Hamish waved his hand dismissively. "No matter. Upper Canada would be too far, even though it is more likely to be inhabited by sensible people."

London, England was certainly not inhabited by sensible people.

At least not in the regions around Hyde Park that the *ton* delighted in frequenting, as if the artificial Serpentine might in any manner rival the brilliance of even the smallest, most unassuming loch in the Highlands.

"Is my brother under the impression that there are no appropriate women in Scotland?" Hamish asked. "Or that he is not already betrothed?"

No woman could be more suitable than Isla McIntyre. She was accomplished, beautiful, and above all, a McIntyre. *And Callum's marriage with her is the only way we can keep Montgomery Castle.*

The pained look on the butler's face appeared again. "I would not want to muse over the duke's reasoning."

Hamish nodded. "Aye. Quite right. It's the sort of thing that would give one a headache."

Not for the first time, Hamish wished the title were his. He would do a far better job of acting honorably than his brother—he always had. If he chided himself for his one-time tardiness; it was not because he craved the attention and accolades that accompanied the title. Perhaps it would matter to members of the *ton* who adored balls and thought a title would give them an advantage when seeking dance partners.

Hamish had never suffered from a dearth of female interest. Apparently, there was something about his broad shoulders, dark hair, and chiseled facial features that caused lassies to exclaim excitedly in his presence. His brother also did not suffer from lack of attention from women. Unfortunately, Callum did not devote attention to his duties.

"My brother cannot be marrying an Englishwoman." Hamish tightened his fingers around the letter, creasing the edge. "He's supposed to marry Lady Isla. Everyone knows that. And this woman is from Norfolk."

Norfolk was hardly the provenance of the *ton's* elite. And how could some lassie who'd grown accustomed to flat plains and banal landscapes possibly expect to feel at home in the Highlands? Likely she would have heart palpitations from viewing so much beauty.

"I can't allow my brother, the only one I have, to destroy his life in this manner. Are future generations of the esteemed Montgomery family supposed to be raised in England?" Hamish scowled.

"It is possible that the duke believes himself to be in love."

"Love?" Hamish sputtered.

Love was a concoction. Hamish knew it. His butler knew it. Unfortunately, Callum must not be aware of it.

God in heaven.

Hamish wasn't going to permit his only sibling, his brother, heir to the title, to marry some English fortune hunter who was not even in possession of a minor aristocratic title. Hamish might always have thought that viscountesses and baronesses could be pompous, but one did rather desire one's only sibling not marry a woman obviously devoid of respectability.

No.

There was only one thing to do, and it did not entail wedding guests.

Hamish rose. He glanced longingly for a moment at his drafting board and the carefully drawn crow-stepped gables, pointed turrets and a luxurious porte-cochère so his client's family would not get wet when they left their carriage to enter their home. His fingers itched to grasp his ruling pen again. This was his first commission, and it needed to be perfect. Still, the design, and all its neo-Gothic glory would have to wait. Family was more important.

"I am going to London," Hamish announced. "Please inform my valet to pack my bags."

Hamish would have to stop the wedding.

Chapter Two

THE FLOORBOARDS CREAKED in a now-familiar rhythm as Flora answered the door, and Georgiana nudged Charlotte. Her sister's face tended to be reserved, and her upcoming nuptials had not changed that, but Georgiana knew she must be delighted.

Georgiana Butterworth rose and fixed a smile on her face. The action was easy to do, since the caller was always the same.

Mama clasped her hands together. "It's the duke! My darling son!"

"You did not birth him, my dear." Their father did not remove his gaze from his leather-bound book.

"That makes him the very best sort of child." Mama cast a stern glance in the direction of Georgiana and Charlotte. "You would not believe the horrors you put me through."

"I am rather surprised my eardrums still function," Papa said. "And I was sequestered in the other side of the house."

"You should have left," Mama said, though Georgiana had the curious sense she was not altogether upset. But then, Georgiana had had the questionable fortune of seeing her mother display a variety of emotions. Her mother was far less distraught than when she contemplated the unfashionableness of her own attire.

Papa's talents did not extend to alchemy, despite his vast knowledge of the works of the obscurest philosophers and theologians, and he did not have the wealth to ensure immaculate attire.

Vicar's daughters were not truly supposed to have a season, no matter the loftiness of the maternal side of the family. Several debutantes had taken it upon themselves to personally inform Georgiana and Charlotte about this breach of unwritten etiquette.

"Men are utterly impossible," Mama said, still gazing at her husband with a smile.

Georgiana resisted the urge to roll her eyes. Her parents were maddeningly fond of each other, despite the fact that most other married couples seemed to deem it fashionable to fling insults at each other. Many society matrons recited the list of their husbands' faults with the same vigor with which they enthused over this year's colors and dress cuts.

The door opened, and the duke ducked his head and entered the room. Homes from the last century might have their charms, but they were scarcely prepared to accommodate tall, broad-shouldered dukes. The furniture seemed rather barer when contrasted against the sumptuous material and rich colors of the duke's attire, and Georgiana wished the spindles between the chairs' legs were not quite as bulky, as if the carpenter had not had confidence in the ability of the chairs to stand upright.

"Did I hear you say men are impossible?" The duke's blue eyes glimmered.

"With the word 'utterly' as emphasis," Papa said casually, raising his head from his book.

Mama's confident smile transformed to horror, and she clutched her hand to her fichu with such vigor it seemed in danger of falling out. Her white cap, laden with frills and flounces in an architecturally unstable manner, *did* slide down, and she grasped it valiantly. "I wasn't referring to you, my dear duke. You are most assuredly not horrible. You are—"

"The antithesis of it," Papa suggested, smoothing his sideburns.

Mama nodded eagerly. "Indeed, the very antithesis of horrible! Even though you do not lack manly characteristics."

From the manner in which her mother's eyes sparkled, Georgiana suspected that might have been a rare understatement.

"You are too kind," the duke said.

Georgiana remembered to dip into a curtsy, and Charlotte and Mama followed while Papa and the duke busied themselves with bows.

Mama rang for Flora to bring tea, just as she did every time the duke visited. The Butterworth family had never been so alert.

Despite the frequency of the duke's visits, they were always strained and short. It must be terrible for him to be surrounded by chaperones when he visited his fiancée. None of the heroes in Loretta Van Lochen's thrilling romances had to put up with lengthy small talk with their beloved's relatives while biting into sweets and balancing saucers filled with hot tea on their knees.

Georgiana glanced back at Charlotte, who had resumed her needlepoint, evidently eager to occupy her fingers when in his presence.

Somehow, her younger sister Charlotte, despite the fact this was her first season and she'd been dismissed as a permanent wallflower by the *ton*'s matrons at Almack's, had managed to land not just a fiancé, but one of the rare ducal variety.

"I wonder when your brother will arrive," Mama said politely.

"My brother?" The duke's normally handsome face reddened.

"Yes."

"Ah." He seemed to recover himself. "I am afraid he cannot come. The man considers even the Border Counties to be too English."

"But you are his only sibling," Georgiana blurted.

"Indeed." The Duke of Vernon bestowed a bland smile.

Mama fluttered her fan with greater force, as if overtaken by his charm.

Well.

She probably had been overcome by it.

His Grace's handsomeness was something even *Matchmaking for Wallflowers*, the scandal sheets most known for criticisms, raved about with regularity.

His blond hair curled in a manner Georgiana was most accustomed to seeing in Venetian depictions of cherubs, though no one seemed to think that an issue. Perhaps it was because his figure managed to be both trim and muscular, and he was reported to wear breeches with a seldom-found grace at Almack's. No doubt the man did not even stuff his stockings to give them an appearance of added muscularity as so many men were forced to do, daunted by the prospect of displaying their lower legs for judgment.

The duke crossed his legs, though Georgiana was certain it was out of discomfort, and not from an urge to flaunt the robust results of his horseback rides through Hyde Park like some athletically inclined peacock.

"Tell me, what is your brother like?" Mama asked. "He is most mysterious. No one in London knows anything about him. Does he have any preferred breakfast foods? I want to make sure he enjoys the wedding breakfast."

"He is really of no concern," the duke said.

Georgiana narrowed her eyes. There were many things Georgiana did not care to discuss, but her sister was not one of them. Charlotte was always a source of great joy, a paragon of virtue to which Georgiana might aspire.

"Ah, he's your twin, is he not?" Papa lifted his head from his Plato. "Perhaps you have a special connection. There are many famous twins. Apollo and Artemis. Romulus and Remus."

"But unlike Romulus, the duke's brother will hardly go about murdering anyone when he arrives for the wedding," Georgiana said with a laugh.

The room stilled, and every gaze scrutinized her. She shifted her position on the sofa. Every movement seemed to draw additional dubiousness, as if they were pondering the possibility she might do something equally inappropriate.

"Not even worth contemplating," Mama said finally.

"Yes," Georgiana said, rather more meekly than when she'd brought up "duke" and "twin" and "murder" with apparently too much casualness.

It was no use stressing she had meant the duke to be quite safe. Now was perhaps a time to be quiet. Nothing could get in the way of her sister's everlasting happiness.

She sighed. Perhaps she was too quick to speak, not willing to limit her opinion to which colors were becoming. Perhaps once Charlotte married, her parents would relax their expectations of her. Perhaps she might continue to design gardens. Other ladies in the gentry had expressed interest after seeing the results of her work for her father's vicarage.

"Why do you say my brother will arrive soon?" The duke's pensive expression had not shifted since Mama had first mentioned his brother's impending visit.

"He wrote me," Mama declared.

The duke blinked. "Wrote *you?*"

"I had to invite him," Mama said. "And he replied."

"How splendid," the duke said faintly.

"Well, I really mustn't get all the credit. You must have invited him first."

"Er—yes."

Charlotte smoothed her muslin gown, though Georgiana wondered whether it was more to mask the trembling of her fingers. "You really shouldn't have done that, Mama. You should have consulted with the duke."

"Oh, nonsense. I didn't even use vellum. Just paper. Though it is good you are concerned with the expense." Mama beamed at the duke. "My daughters are both very economical. Quite a good quality in a future wife."

"Ah, he's already been convinced," Papa said, and the duke flushed.

Georgiana cringed, conscious he must be assessing the shabbiness of their surroundings. Probably he did not want Georgiana's parents to speculate he was only marrying Charlotte for her ability to scrimp and save. The quality was unlikely to be one he needed.

The duke shifted his legs over the faded Persian carpet.

"You do appear ill," Mama said. "Let me fetch Flora. She always knows what to do. Perhaps some tea will revive you. Tea always revives everyone. Who knew pouring hot water over leaves would be so splendid?"

"Apparently lots of people knew," Georgiana said. "In Asia."

"Does Asia count, dear?" Mama gave a triumphant smile, as if Georgiana could not possibly counter it.

Georgiana frowned and was about to reply, but the duke interrupted her. "I-I should return home."

"Naturally. You must desire to prepare for your brother's arrival. The wedding's in two days. He's bound to arrive today."

"Er—yes." The duke headed for the door, then stopped abruptly, remembering to bow.

Georgiana's family descended once again into bows and curtsies, and Georgiana was relieved when he'd left.

Charlotte frowned. "I really wish you hadn't written him, Mama."

"Nonsense. You don't mean that," their mother replied, though an uncertain note had entered her voice.

Chapter Three

THE SUN MIGHT BE SETTING, casting pink and orange light over the excessively ornate buildings, but thankfully the coachman did not succumb to any sentimental urgings and slow his speed. The hired post chaise moved briskly through Smithfield Market and entered Mayfair. Finally, it halted, and Hamish leaped onto the pavement, not waiting for the coachman to assist him.

His brother's townhouse loomed before him, wedged into a row of neatly maintained homes on Grosvenor Square. The man didn't even have a garden, and the stretch of lawn on the square seemed an imperfect substitute. Why did Callum insist on living here, when he might have an entire castle at his disposal perched on a craggy mountaintop that trounced any Palladian design in magnificence?

His chest panged. Their parents had gone to their graves assuming that their eldest son would marry the neighbors' daughter, as had Lord and Lady McIntyre themselves. Dear Isla was expecting to be made a duchess. Her *brother* was expecting her to become a duchess, and one didn't go about irritating Wolfe, especially when their properties touched.

Callum should be grateful his life had been so neatly arranged and not strive to make it complicated by making promises to lassies, no matter how fetching they might look.

Hamish strode toward the portico. He knew what would happen next: the butler would announce him, and his brother would express surprise he'd made the long journey.

Perhaps Callum and he would call on the family the next morning, and he could attempt to make forced conversation over whatever ridiculous drinks the English served. Likely they would give him some tea. The English *ton* seemed delighted in pouring hot water over dried herbs from the Orient and declaring it a delicacy. Hamish huffed. Nothing could compare to a good Scottish whisky.

Perhaps Callum would worry he hadn't informed Hamish about the wedding, allowing his twin to learn about the ill-advised ceremony from a stranger. Hamish tightened his fists, as if to brace himself for the inevitable argument.

Hamish had spent years working to rectify the estate's finances. Now that they'd regained their wealth, they couldn't lose their manor house. What was a dukedom without an estate? Lord McIntyre had bought the mortgage years ago with the agreement that Callum could keep the estate if he married Lord McIntyre's daughter.

Hamish's chest tightened. Perhaps Callum would insist he'd fallen victim to Cupid's invisible arrow. That seemed the only thing that could inspire his brother to make such a disastrous decision.

Unless the English lassie has something on him.

It hadn't been enough for Callum to battle the French. He'd then had to ensconce himself in some den of disrepute. Who knew the criminals he might encounter?

London might swarm with arrogant people who held the mistaken belief that these streets surpassed that of every town, every hamlet, every meadow in Britain, but the city also remained the favorite dwelling of ruffians, no doubt gleeful at being so near to those desirous of funds to maintain their contemptible conduct.

His cousin Gerard had told him about the unsavory practices of the Duke of Belmonte, one of London's most menacing men, despite the respectability of his title. The duke had sent a henchman after Gerard when he had inherited a loan from his mother, one she'd signed in her final months of illness, when anyone with any sense would know she was in no position to make financial decisions.

Perhaps Callum had fallen victim to him as well, and Belmonte was insisting on the marriage for some perverse purpose.

Hamish quickened his steps. He was here now. They'd figure something out.

Except—

Hamish halted his stride.

It was possible speaking with his brother would not be an ideal method of ending the engagement. Any conversation might lead to insistences that Hamish vow not to interfere. Perhaps instead Hamish might convince Callum's *bride* to end the engagement.

With any luck, Callum would never know he'd interfered, and he could play devoted brother. He might even pick up some handkerchiefs from Savile Row on his way back. Hamish grinned and returned to the coach, whistling *Scots, Who Have.*

If the coachman thought it curious Hamish hadn't used the conveniently placed brass door knocker, he didn't say anything.

"One more stop, I'm afraid," Hamish told the coachman.

"Very well." The coachman reloaded Hamish's bag into the post chaise. "Where to?"

Hamish grabbed the wedding invitation and read the address of the Butterworth residence, and soon they were on their way. The sun toppled farther downward, turning the buildings a crimson shade that appropriately resembled the depths of Hades. The horses dashed toward the address. Hamish removed a small purse and stepped from the carriage. This street was narrower and shrouded in darkness. It did not surround a grand square, much less one with a park, and the carriage blocked the path.

"Better return," Hamish said. "I'm not sure how long this will take. You can give my bag to His Grace's servants."

"If you're certain—"

"I am."

The coachman nodded and coaxed the horses into a trot. The distance between the two places was miniscule, even if the change in affluence was not, and Hamish would be able to return on foot.

He'd been curious what sort of home his brother's intended resided in.

At least the building was devoid of Grecian columns and urns on its facade, though knowing the English, that meant the family was not as wealthy as they should be. The building wasn't on Grosvenor Square, and Hamish knew enough about the *ton* to know this was suboptimal.

He shrugged. Why people should desire to live in a series of identical townhouses was beyond him. The nice thing about Scotland—one of the many, very, very nice things about Scotland—was that there was plenty of room for castles, and no one was there to note if one's turret was misshapen.

Not that any of his turrets were misshapen.

Hamish paced the street. He needed to formulate a plan. He could hardly barge inside and demand the family release his brother from an engagement to their daughter. They knew the consequences of a broken engagement. The woman would be unlikely to make an equally advantageous match again, but Hamish pushed away his sudden guilt.

The Butterworth family had obviously schemed to get their daughter betrothed to a duke, and they were unlikely to be coaxed to break the engagement. They would not see his position as younger brother to the duke as sufficiently intimidating.

Hamish's best chance lay in the lass herself, and he wrapped his hands around his purse, feeling the familiar shape of the gold coins. He couldn't permit this woman to marry his brother and he couldn't find her a new husband, but he could give her something else: freedom.

Wasn't freedom something some women craved? With any good luck, she'd read Mary Wollstonecraft. Perhaps she'd even devoured books on the French and American revolutions. Younger people had a delightful tendency to be idealistic.

A dim light flickered in an upstairs window, and he held his breath. A flash of long auburn hair appeared and the curved, unmistakable figure of a woman.

Miss Charlotte Butterworth.

Excitement thrummed through him, and he thanked the faeries for looking out for him even in this dreadful compilation of closely placed dwellings that was London.

Hamish had never considered breaking into a home before, but then, his brother had never announced a marital engagement to an inappropriate woman before either.

Coins shifted in Hamish's purse. He hoped they would be a sufficient bribe to call off the wedding.

Miss Butterworth must be a veritable Cleopatra. Or Venus in one of her more seductive guises. Why else would his brother cast aside centuries of proper Scottish behavior to run off with an Englishwoman? Hamish shuddered to think what their kilt-wearing, bagpipe-playing ancestors would think about Callum's behavior.

Light glowed from the window, as if Hades himself were inside.

There was a perfectly good balcony there and a just as excellent tree. How could fate have provided these two disparate things so close together without intent?

Hamish's lips quirked into a smile.

Callum had abdicated any right for his family members to act with decorum after he'd so recklessly tied himself to this woman and whatever wretched family she possessed.

He swung his gaze around, striving to maintain nonchalance, but no one was there. Darkness shrouded the sky, and even the stars and moon were absent, a perhaps not unusual occurrence in foggy, filthy London.

He removed his top hat and tailcoat and hung them upon a branch. The wind wafted about his shirt sleeves, and he loosened his cravat. Then he dashed toward the tree, pushed against the trunk to catapult himself higher, and clasped the lowest branch. For a moment he swayed, then he pulled himself up onto a stout branch. He inhaled the scent of leaves and bark and worked his way along the branch toward the building. Finally, when he neared the balcony, he swung toward it.

He smiled. If Lady McIntyre could see him now, he could assure her his instinct to clamber up trees and his years of practice had all been worthwhile.

Thud.

His feet hit the stone, but the next sound was rather more high-pitched, as ceramic scraped together and the heavy scent of hyacinths inundated the air.

He must have collided with a potted plant.

God in heaven.

His venture onto the balcony had been noisier than he'd intended. He placed the hyacinth gently back onto its saucer. Evidently, Miss Butterworth liked flowers. The fact wasn't precisely unpleasant, and he felt another trickle of guilt.

No matter. Even Persephone had been the goddess of spring growth and she'd been the queen of the underworld.

He stretched his shoulders, enjoying the sensation of the linen brushing against his back, freed from his constricting coat, and strode toward the balcony door.

In normal situations, he would never enter an unmarried woman's chamber, lest she or some conspiring parent declare her compromised.

Especially in such an undressed manner.

Still, this was different. Miss Butterworth was already engaged to his brother, and since Callum was the larger prize, he doubted she would scream. And if she did? If he were forced to marry her instead of having his brother marry her, he would still be fulfilling his Montgomery duty. Better to sacrifice any hope of marital bliss for himself than the well-being of future Montgomerys.

Marrying anyone, much less an Englishwoman whom he'd never met, was dreadful to imagine. Still, he would take that risk. Sullying the Montgomery name would never be an option.

A CLATTER AND THEN shuffling filtered through the balcony door, and Georgiana raised her head from the latest Loretta Van Lochen novel. It sounded as if some animal were outside, and she smiled. This animal seemed of the large variety, given the heaviness of the thuds. Were any of her fine neighbors in the habit of keeping pigs?

The handle of the balcony door rattled, and Georgiana's good mood vanished. Pigs, for all their porcine charm, would not be inclined to test door handles and they wouldn't, she remembered too late, be able to climb onto a balcony.

Heavens.

She'd forgotten to lock the balcony door.

Georgiana's hands shook as she slammed her book shut and shoved it onto her bedside table. She cursed her earlier instinct to open the door, as if she could possibly inhale the scent of lilacs and apple blossoms like in Norfolk.

The door flew open, and a man strolled into the room. His ivory shirt contrasted against the inky sky behind him. The man was tall, and his shoulders broad.

The only man who called on her in Norfolk was the curate, and he'd only arrived at appropriate calling hours armed with appropriate conversation about weather patterns.

This man was no curate.

At least not the simpering sort to which she was accustomed.

The stranger's skin was of the sun-kissed variety, and she wondered how anyone could possibly think the hue unfashionable. This man seemed to belong in the midst of nature, away from Mayfair's long rows of houses with their absence of gardens. A well-formed column could never rival the magnificence of a simple tree, even if the column were the Corinthian sort, with all manner of exquisite, never-falling leaves to adorn it.

She swallowed hard, though the action seemed more difficult than normal, perhaps because of the frantic beating of her heart.

Everything about this man was scandalous, and he strode toward her. He directed Azurean eyes at her, and she shivered under his curious gaze. His loose cravat fluttered indecently in the wind, and his thin shirt hardly masked the man's abundance of muscles.

His attire, what little there was of it, seemed of too high a quality for him to be a thief, though perhaps he was the successful sort.

Georgiana drew back in her bed. The pillows' softness was of no comfort to her now, and she despised the manner in which the bed dipped in the middle.

This was when fear should be rushing toward her, but instead she stared, transfixed at the Adonis before her. The man's face was chiseled, as if one of the statues in the National Gallery had come to life, as if somebody had decided that a man of such exquisite masculinity could not remain of stone.

She pulled her covers over her, conscious she should do something, but he curled his lips. "That's no protection, lassie."

The man's Scottish accent took her by surprise. Scotland might be part of Great Britain, but it was far enough away from London to be somewhat of a rarity. The duke had a slight accent, but this was thicker, more sonorous, more musical, as if his very words, and their lilting tone, mimicked the rolling hills of Scotland about which every Scot seemed to rhapsodize.

The bell pull.

Reaching it would require leaving her bed.

The man would have to see her in her night rail.

Never mind.

She scrambled from her bed and lurched toward the bell pull.

"Not so fast, lassie." The stranger's hand clamped about hers with all the force of steel, though the warmth of his skin was most unmetallic. She'd eliminated the possibility that the man was a specter. Specters weren't supposed to feel so utterly lifelike.

She struggled in his grasp, conscious of a heavy oak scent, conjuring everything removed from her parents' dainty vicarage in Norfolk and their even daintier rented townhouse on the outskirts of Mayfair. Protesting seemed impossible, but Georgiana refused to be intimidated by the impossible. With all her might she stepped on his foot.

"Ow!" The man yelped.

The man swept her into his arms, lifting her off the ground. The coldness of his shirt somehow did not suffice in preventing heat from swirling through her, and the thin linen seemed an absurd barrier against the firm chest it attempted to cover.

Chest hairs curled in an intriguing manner below his loose cravat, and his face loomed above her, darkened by a smattering of facial hair.

She had to remind herself she was terrified. Something about the feel of his arms about her seemed almost reassuring, as if he could protect her against anything in the world. She kicked her legs all the same, conscious of the utter impropriety of the man's actions and completely aware of her parents' presence in the townhouse.

In a few expedient strides, he marched her to a chair and settled her into it, pressing her against the ornate crest rail and making her wish it were not quite as elaborate. The chair's arms poked her body, the discomfort not lessened by the soft manchettes.

"I would advise you to be quiet," he said, still speaking in that exasperatingly magical manner.

"I would advise you to leave the room." The words seemed to come out an octave higher than she intended, her diaphragm evidently equally flummoxed by his presence, and he smirked.

She did her best glower, but the stern expression was evidently more effective on her younger cousins than on him. Her heart pitched, like a captain striving to steady a ship in the midst of a hurricane, and her gaze fell on a silver candlestick on a nearby sideboard.

Chapter Four

GOD IN HEAVEN.

The woman was divine.

The night rail was sheer, and Miss Charlotte Butterworth did not seem conscious of the manner in which the candlelight flickered over the fabric, devoid of pesky stays or a shift to hamper his view.

Hamish forced his gaze to not linger on her chest or the delightful manner in which her hips curved. Unfortunately, the woman's face was not devoid of charm. Wide-set eyes glared at him, and exquisitely shaped lips veered into a frown. Likely similar musings on the woman's beauty had compelled his brother to impetuously propose to her.

"Who are you? And what on earth are you doing?" The woman tossed her hair, and auburn curls rippled down her back.

Her lustrous locks reached her waist, and Hamish had a definite urge to run his hand through them. No doubt they would feel silky beneath his fingers.

He shook his head. Most likely the trip had simply been excessively dry, and her glossy locks seemed excessively appealing. Carriage journeys were not known for their comfort, and despite the coachman's excellent driving skills, this latest trip had not deviated from that standard. No wonder his fingers longed to touch something soft.

Hamish was made of sterner stuff than his brother and he reached for his bag of coin. The woman would be looking rather less fearful soon.

All he had to do was convince her to accept the money and not marry his brother. Then he could go merrily on his way back down the tree, tuck himself away in his castle in his beloved Scotland, and continue designing glorious architectural creations. He beamed, though the woman drew back. Evidently, she viewed his happiness with suspicion.

"Leave this room," she said sternly. "At once."

"No."

Fear flickered over her face, and Hamish forced away the guilt that surged through him. At least he should not frighten her.

No matter.

This woman was a common title seeker. A petty peon. A tufthunter.

She longed to be a duchess and have a significant allowance.

The sun might have set, and they might be relying on candlelight to see, but her hair still seemed a most marvelous and vibrant red.

His brother had always seemed more intrigued by fragile appearing blondes who looked as if they should have the same precautions bestowed upon them as the most delicate porcelain, no matter how characterless it rendered them. Those were the women who reigned London's ballrooms. The one time Hamish had been in the capital he'd nearly expired from dullness. No matter Bonaparte's faults, he'd at least provided a wonderful excuse to abandon the season.

Well.

This woman seemed most unlike the others. His gaze drifted to an open book by her bedside. *The Dashing Pirate and the Spanish Princess.* He smirked at the sensational title. No point musing over the evolution of Callum's taste. The freckles on her skin made it impossible to compare her complexion to milk-and-rose blossoms, or whatever the fashionable comparison was these days. Callum had not skimped on the inappropriateness: her face was rounder, her mouth wider, and her lips fuller.

The latter fact might have some merits, and Hamish smiled.

"What are you thinking?" Suspicion filled the lass's voice.

"You're not a blonde and you have many freckles."

She gasped, and her eyes darkened in obvious fury.

"Not that you're not pretty," he said, pondering again the warmth exuded from her auburn hair and freckled skin. "Just rather less—er—conventionally so."

"Leave my chambers immediately." She gripped the arms of her chair, as if half expecting him to haul her off again.

She needn't worry. He could resist the temptation of soft curves in his arms and a vanilla scent. He was stronger than his brother.

Hamish reached for his purse, and the lassie's face paled. If he hadn't seen her moving about earlier, he might have assumed her to have been taken deathly ill. Painters would find the paleness of her skin, with its softness, an appropriate likeness for any portrayal of a death scene.

"I'll scream," she said.

He raised his eyebrow. "Then you would have screamed a long time ago."

Her cheeks flushed.

She didn't need to explain.

They both knew her reputation would be compromised if she were found with a man in her chambers. It was the sort of thing that would cause servants to gossip, particularly if they were disturbed from the comfort of their beds or the hearth in the kitchen.

"Well then," she said, her voice wobbling, "I'll hurt you."

She touched a silver candlestick, and in the next moment she brandished it before her like a weapon.

He blinked, but he hadn't conjured the image. She still brandished the candlestick at him.

He'd never appreciated a candlestick's function as a defense weapon before, but the long, thick silver looked decidedly threatening.

Not that he would be harmed by it.

Hamish prided himself on his wrestling ability and he wouldn't be foiled by something intended as a decorative item. "Be careful, lassie. You don't want someone to take you up on the offer for a fight."

"Did you come to my chamber just to argue with me?"

He gave her a slow smile. "I can think of more pleasant things to do with you, lassie. But then, so has my brother."

This time her mouth dropped open, and for a strange second confusion marched over her face.

The fact was absurd, and Hamish frowned. "Don't tell me you've forgotten him so quickly."

"You're Lord Hamish." Miss Butterworth lowered the candlestick in a tentative gesture, and the movement shifted her night rail, revealing a delicious new sliver of skin.

He forced his gaze away. "Aye, so I am."

"And you think I'm—" She paused abruptly and placed the candlestick back on the sideboard.

Hamish waited, but the lassie had evidently not decided to speak any further. She had the gall to raise her eyebrow, and her right foot tapped against the floor.

Her right, *bare* foot. The shape was narrow and accompanied by a high arch, small, delicate-appearing toes and an ankle that swept inward in a graceful manner—

He shifted his gaze to the candlestick. Her feet didn't matter. After tonight, he'd never see her again. "I know you're planning to marry my brother. And I won't permit it."

"Why is that?"

"Because you're not suitable."

"Is that so?" She tossed her hair, shifting the auburn strands. Some locks appeared dark amaretto and others cognac under the golden glow of the flickering candlelight.

He scrutinized her. The action was no hardship.

Now the lass was obviously no longer reciting prayers to herself or thinking of manners in which to dismember him, Hamish could see that not only was she in the possession of a delightful abundance of freckles, she also had dimples.

But then, this woman was not someone whom his brother had selected for companionship for a waltz or to wander with through a secluded garden; this woman was to be his wife.

Perhaps his brother possessed more sophisticated tastes than Hamish had given him credit for. Hamish's lips twitched.

That was unlikely. Clearly, Miss Butterworth was simply cleverer than he'd initially imagined.

"I'm going to offer you money." Hamish held out the bag of coin, and it jangled in the quiet of the room.

The lass drew back. "You can't be serious."

"Oh, but I am."

"How much do you plan to pay?"

"Enough money to last your whole life."

She gasped.

Hamish could have taken less money with him, but the wedding was planned. The invitations had been sent. He couldn't ask her to back out of an engagement at this point without being conscious that her reputation would be permanently smeared, at least until some poor soul agreed to marry her.

"That's not as much money as I will have if I marry him," Miss Butterworth said, her voice defiant.

Hamish forced himself to shrug nonchalantly. This was the important part of the negotiation. He needed to appeal to what she desired. Perhaps it might be beneficial if he knew her better, but instead he launched into a now familiar speech.

Miss Butterworth was not the first woman who'd desired to wed his brother, overlooking the man's practical betrothal to Isla McIntyre, though she was the first woman to send out wedding invitations. The latter fact did not speak well of any future ability to manage the castle's household budget. Everyone knew no one invited guests to a wedding. Marriages were a legal matter, something that did not require a multitude of gawkers. Large weddings were confined to royals, and though his brother might possess a castle, it was thankfully not associated with Britain's royal family.

"The money will give you your freedom," Hamish said, watching the lass carefully.

The word freedom did seem to change her expression. She seemed more thoughtful, and something sparked in her eyes.

"You can have a cottage by the sea. Just take the money," he said.

"I refuse to do so."

"You don't need a fancy title to be happy."

She smirked. "Are you saying that because you don't have one?"

Warmth clambered up his neck and seemed to be debating whether to extend to his cheeks. Despite Hamish's embarrassment, he squared his shoulders. "He's no good for you."

"Nonsense. And why are you speaking poorly of him? He's your sibling."

Hamish had no desire to speak ill of his brother to some woman he'd only just met. He didn't desire to criticize him at all. Callum possessed ample charm, and Hamish had spent merry evenings with him.

That didn't mean he'd permit Callum to destroy the legacy generations of the Montgomery family had created. Their sacrifices shouldn't be for naught. His father shouldn't be rolling about in his grave, agonized by his elder son's poor choices and Hamish's inability to prevent them.

No.

That wouldn't do.

Hamish might have been born eight minutes later than Callum, but he'd be damned if he'd permit Callum to squander the Montgomery estate on some impoverished lassie from Nor-folk, no matter how appealing her auburn locks.

"Look," Hamish said. "Just take the money. You don't want to move to Scotland. It's cold there. And if you think it rains too much in England, you *don't* want to venture north."

She smiled. "I'll pack my umbrella."

Dash it, he was being serious. Now was not the time for smiles.

It certainly wasn't the time for her brown eyes to sparkle.

He was certain he wasn't supposed to find brown a very interesting color. No royal placed brown jewels on their crowns: he was certain brown jewels didn't even exist. Brown was a color relegated to muddy patches the grass could not cover. And yet on Miss Butterworth, the color did not seem like something that should be dismissed in the slightest.

"I don't mind the rain," she said.

The lass would probably enjoy wandering about the High-lands after all, undaunted by the steepness of the peaks. *God in heaven.* She was supposed to leap at the chance to obtain such easily accessible funds. That had been the plan.

"And I find balls far overrated," she continued.

"Even Almack's?" he asked, thinking of his brother's habit of frequenting that establishment.

"Especially Almack's."

He stepped toward her.

The lass's eyes continued to glimmer, and he forced away images of twirling her upon the dance floor.

She couldn't really be so loyal to Callum. She had seemed intrigued by the possibility of freedom. Her eyes hadn't glazed in a calf-like manner and her hand hadn't once ventured to her chest, as if to stifle the sound of a thundering heart, when speaking about him. She'd been calm, collected, and almost businesslike.

An idea occurred to him, and he grasped her hands. Their unobtrusive shape did not lessen the jolt of heat, jolt of sheer energy that cascaded through him as their skin touched. His heart thumped wildly, and he pulled her closer to him.

Her eyes widened, and for an absurd moment he contemplated simply staring into them, musing on the wonders of their umber color, undisturbed by hints of green or flecks of gold.

"Don't marry him." Hamish lowered his head and brushed his mouth against hers, claiming her succulent, rose-colored lips.

They tasted marvelous.

They melded with his, and he was transported far from London, far from the Highlands, to some heavenly region he'd never before experienced.

He clutched his arms around her slender waist and delved his hands through her luscious locks. They were every bit as glossy as he'd imagined. The finest silkworms would blush at the crudity of their creations were they to ever encounter a single strand of her hair.

It's not supposed to feel this good.

He pulled himself from her lips, eager to regain some control and quell the confusion raging through his body. This was a woman who'd maneuvered his brother, a man who should have known better, into a marriage.

He raised his chin and gazed into startled, awestruck eyes. "You can't love him."

Chapter Five

SHE WAS BEING KISSED.

She was blissfully conscious of the sensation of his lips, of his tongue, and the manner his hands moved over her body, as if seeking to memorize it.

She inhaled the Scotsman's masculine scent, so different from the cologne-spurting dandies prevalent in the *ton*. No floral compilation distracted her.

Lips brushed against hers in a delicious, ever-changing rhythm, more satisfying than that by any continental composer.

His arms had appeared muscular even in the dim light cast by the flickering candles, but now that no space separated them, the sensation was stronger.

Her sister's intended brother-in-law had scrambled up the wall to enter her room through the balcony.

And yet, though Georgiana knew she should pull away, knew this was one of those situations that did deserve a slap, pulling away seemed impossible.

Were they to stop kissing, they would likely have to discuss the kiss, and since Georgiana had never been kissed before, she wasn't certain of the appropriate etiquette.

And the worst thing was—

It was pleasant.

Ridiculously, gloriously pleasant.

But then he thought she was marrying his brother. The fact soared through her mind, and she pressed her hands against his shirt, resisting the urge to contemplate the firm muscles beneath the linen, and shoved him away.

He moved instantly, and his hair appeared more tousled than before, and she realized it was because her hands had touched it. His skin was now flushed, and his eyes appeared disoriented.

"You kissed me," she said, despising the confusion in her voice.

He hardened his expression and roamed his gaze over her body. "You enjoyed it."

She flinched. "Why did you do it?"

He smiled, and unlike during his kiss, there seemed nothing pleasant about the manner in which his lips curled. His expression turned stony. "You shouldn't marry my brother."

"Oh," she squeaked. "That's—"

Mad? Insane? A flurry of words invaded her mind. She had no intention of wedding the duke, but then she was not engaged to him.

She considered telling him she was merely his brother's betrothed's sister, but she didn't want him to pester Charlotte. Her sister didn't need to feel unwelcome in her new family. She must already feel overwhelmed by the duke's impeccable status.

Her sister was so good. If she thought marrying the duke would bring him harm, she might be convinced to break off the engagement, no matter the horrific consequences she would face.

Formerly betrothed women could not easily find another fiancé. Everyone seemed to think chaperones were laxer after their charges had rings firmly on their fingers, and if Charlotte's betrothal were to end, people would practically expect her to depart suddenly to Switzerland for a months-long health cure. No other man would desire to marry her if the heritage of any resulting child would be forever questioned.

Georgiana would not allow Charlotte to be the subject of such malicious gossip. No way would she permit Charlotte to be persuaded to abandon her engagement.

Georgiana raised her chin to an angle that did not feel the least bit natural now and rallied her voice to evoke severity. "You need to leave."

"Are you certain?" he drawled. "What with all the kisses?"

Anger inundated her, replacing all the pleasant sensations that were still fluttering through her. "You're an abomination."

She studied him. The man's likeness to his brother was relegated to similarly straight noses and defined chins. The duke's brother's hair was dark, and it didn't curl in any manner, much less an angelic one.

His shoulders seemed broader, more intimidating, though the duke had never stood as close to her as his brother did now. Once again her nostrils flared, acting against her will, as if enticed by the scent of manliness.

She jerked her head away.

There was nothing the least bit admirable about him, she reminded herself.

"Do you despise your brother?" she asked.

His blue eyes widened, and he stepped back. "Of course not."

"Then why would you deny him the woman he loves?"

"Loves?" The man's voice wobbled, as if he were musing the concept. "He loves you?"

Well. He loved Charlotte. Of that Georgiana was certain. Why else would he marry her? Even Georgiana knew Charlotte was an unlikely choice, despite her sister's sweetness and beauty. He must have been compelled by love.

"What greater force is there?" she asked.

Lord Hamish scowled, and for a moment Georgiana thought he might begin listing scientific elements or weapons. The latter seemed particularly plausible. Wasn't the man supposed to idealize Scotland's medieval heritage? Scotsmen had a peculiar ability to remain in the past, despite its unpleasantness.

Personally, Georgiana preferred the present, if not precisely this incarnation of it.

She glanced toward the door. "My parents might hear you."

"Then I'll declare you compromised, and you won't be able to marry my brother."

She blinked. "But then you'll have to marry me."

"Aye. Perhaps you're correct." The words came out in a much smaller sound, and Georgiana tried to not let her heart drop.

It shouldn't matter that the thought of marrying her brought reason to a mind so uncontrolled by it. After all, she had no desire to marry him either. The man had definite impossible tendencies. No sane man would clamber up the wall of a townhouse.

It was just—

Georgiana had thought she would be betrothed by now. Her governesses had warned her that her auburn hair was unfashionable and might remind some gentlemen of witches, but Georgiana hadn't thought she would find herself with no prospects in sight at the close of her third season.

Everyone had said this was a good time to be a debutante. Men were no longer riding off to war, their epaulets fluttering and their medals gleaming under the sun. Yet the men who returned from the continent and beyond seemed disinclined to marry, favoring the chance to indulge in the pleasures they'd denied themselves in the past. The need to have an heir seemed less urgent when they were no longer dodging cannonballs, and gaming halls seemed more reliable sources of retreat from memories of the war than wedding breakfasts.

But perhaps Georgiana had been wrong, and they'd simply found her distasteful, despite her mother's insistence that Georgiana attend a finishing school in the hopes of making a good match. The good match never appeared, and now a man who had just been kissing her was grimacing at the prospect of spending additional time with her.

"You should leave," Georgiana said, and this time the duke's brother nodded solemnly.

"Think about the money," he said. "If it is a question of more—"

"It isn't," Georgiana said tersely.

Surprise lit his eyes, though unfortunately the emotion did not induce speechlessness. "The duke is betrothed to someone else. He is supposed to marry Lady Isla McIntyre. Her estate borders ours."

The words ricocheted through her. It wasn't the first time she'd heard the duke was engaged, but she'd dismissed it as a rumor. After all, if the duke were truly engaged, he wouldn't have proposed to Charlotte.

But this was the duke's own brother. This was a man who knew the duke's supposed other fiancée.

She squared her shoulders. Lord Hamish's words didn't matter. Perhaps it was even more romantic that the duke had chosen her sister over a more sensible choice. Wasn't that the sort of thing Loretta Van Lochen would write about in her delightful stories? The duke had given his heart to Charlotte, no matter the consequences.

"It doesn't matter," she insisted. "He doesn't love her. Obviously."

"I see you are not to be convinced." The duke's brother swept into a bow. The gesture seemed ridiculous after he'd barreled through all boundaries by breaking into her chamber via the balcony, but she descended into a curtsy.

What could she do?

In two days her sister would marry the duke, and they would no doubt encounter one another at all manner of family gatherings.

Perhaps her sister would move to Scotland to become duchess of an estate in the Highlands, but Georgiana intended to visit her, despite the unpleasantness of her sister's new family.

Lord Hamish opened the door and slipped outside, and Georgiana was left with the sensation of her heart still beating with a great force like a drummer boy calling troops to a battle that had already been lost.

Chapter Six

HAMISH TRAMPED DOWN the tree, grasping the rough bark and branches. Leaves showered over him, perhaps loosened from his recent ascent, and twigs tore at his attire with the ferocity of Bonaparte's Grande Armée. The distance from the ground seemed larger and underscored the absurdity of his earlier action. A strong breeze rippled over him, as if urging him to catapult to the pavement.

Hamish did not fall.

Not that it mattered.

He'd humiliated himself before the woman determined to become his sister-in-law. What would it matter if he spent the rest of his time in London hobbling on one leg?

Evidently, Callum's fiancée was sufficiently enamored of his brother to not accept Hamish's generous offer. The lady was mad. Didn't she know Hamish controlled the finances for the estate? Everything might belong to Callum, but Hamish was the person who occupied himself with it. Did Miss Butterworth imagine Hamish would give her a generous allowance?

Never.

If Miss Butterworth desired to become a duchess, she would have to satisfy herself with being the worst dressed one. He'd hardly want to wager a lifetime on the ability of his brother to interest himself in her. Callum was often on *Matchmaking for Wallflowers'* list of *Rogues to Avoid*, and Hamish didn't want to imagine how Miss Butterworth had trapped him into marriage.

How terrible that his brawny, charming brother could have been felled by a woman not in possession of a title, and given the shabby state of the townhouse in which she lived, not even in possession of a fortune. Most likely she'd confused him with her freckles and feistiness.

Hamish's feet touched the ground, and he grabbed his hat and hastened from the townhouse. Unfortunately, that did not diminish the newly found habit of having Miss Butterworth occupy his mind. He dashed toward Grosvenor Square. The last thing he needed was for some helpful neighbor or servant to spot him climbing from her chambers and insist he'd compromised her.

Life would be wretched indeed, were he forced to marry her.

The streets widened, the houses became taller, and Hamish soon strode up the steps to his brother's townhouse. He grimaced. How could Callum prefer living here to a castle? There wasn't even a moat, and Hamish remained unimpressed by the faux columns someone had attached to the façade in place of actual architectural uniqueness. Why be inspired by the pagan temples of people who'd once conquered Britain, when one could have the best of actual British architecture? Hamish craved his drafting paper and ruling pen.

Lights gleamed from the ground floor. Was his brother unaware candles could be both lit and blown out? He'd have to gift him some candle douters for Christmas. No wonder Callum's expenses remained outrageous.

Hamish clasped hold of the brass knocker, shaped like some damned Roman deity adorned with an equally brass and ludicrous laurel wreath.

The door swung open.

Hmph. Clearly Callum had an efficient butler, or perhaps that was an advantage of the lack of sprawling space.

When the door was fully open, no servant greeted him.

It was his brother.

The man appeared the same as always. His height mirrored Hamish's, and his build consisted of a similar muscularity. He was attired in a black tailcoat and trousers, a white shirt and cravat. Hamish knew better than to think his brother's restraint in palate had anything to do with a sober worldview. His cravat knot alone possessed an unnecessary flourish, the work of a valet whose technical prowess with an iron could likely be put to better uses than his brother's habiliments. Their nursemaids and neighbors had referred to Callum's flaxen hair as angelic, but now his curls were arranged in a fashionable coiffure, as if he'd just had them trimmed.

No doubt for the wedding.

Beyond Callum, elegant crystal chandeliers dangled from the ceiling, polished black-and-white tiles that differed from the rough stones of Montgomery Castle gleamed on the floor, and oil paintings of scantily clad gods and goddesses, rather than Scottish ancestors, hung in gilt frames.

"What a wonderful surprise." Callum spread his lips into a smile Hamish did not for one second believe was derived from happiness.

"It shouldn't be," Hamish said. "Since you marry in two days."

Callum flinched. "Yes. I'm delighted."

"So delighted you couldn't tell me about it?"

This time Callum merely smiled, evidently conscious no words could accurately express his emotions and allow him to remain polite.

"Are you going to invite me in?" Hamish asked.

"You seemed to have no trouble inviting yourself this far."

Some statements required no response, and Hamish sauntered inside. The place was modern; not a single medieval weapon or stag's head about. The foyer's ceilings stretched twenty feet high, an allocation of space hardly beneficial in winter. His brother's questionable judgment did not limit itself to brides.

"Please, let me show you to your room." Callum patted him on the back with the suavity of a member of the House of Lords seeking to obtain votes for a project.

"You anticipated my arrival?"

"Naturally," Callum said smoothly, with the same ease with which he'd always successfully lied to their cooks as a child, when they'd questioned him over the oddly low supply of sugar.

"How clairvoyant." Hamish didn't bother to mask the sarcasm from his voice.

His brother gave a maddening shrug, as if Callum had any cause to be modest. "Your coach driver presented himself to my servants. And—er—my future mother-in-law sent you an invitation."

"At your request?"

Callum gave a tight smile and busied himself with studying the paintings that dotted the corridor, even though Hamish was certain it must have occurred to him before to look at them.

"Where were you just now?" Callum said, changing the subject.

Hamish hesitated.

Telling his brother he'd sneaked into the room of his brother's betrothed to attempt to bribe her so she wouldn't marry him was information unlikely to endear him to Callum.

"I just wanted to go on a stroll," Hamish said, keeping his tone light.

"To admire the capital?" Callum's lips twitched, and for a moment they may as well have been fifteen, chatting in between cricket innings.

"To wonder at its lack of charm."

"London is a pleasant city."

"Our forefathers would roll about in their graves if they heard you say that," Hamish said.

"Then it would give them some excitement. It must be dull for them to stay constantly still."

"You are supposed to marry Isla McIntyre," Hamish said, using his sternest voice.

Callum seemed unfazed. "I suppose I can't now. Even you wouldn't condone bigamy."

"Of course not," Hamish stammered. Still, his mind drifted to a certain auburn-headed woman. That kiss had been damn good. Contemplating that kiss would be far more pleasant than this conversation. Despite everything, he found the corners of his lips veering dangerously high. He might even be smiling.

Callum tilted his head, and his always intelligent eyes narrowed. "You haven't—"

"Haven't what?"

"You haven't met anyone?"

"Nonsense." Hamish raised his chin and rested his hands on his hips, but his limbs felt unnaturally stiff and heavier than normal.

"There was just something in your gaze—"

"There wasn't," Hamish said curtly.

"Right." Callum sighed. "How is your commission?"

"Brilliant."

"It's for a baronet?"

"A *baron*," Hamish said.

Callum nodded, and his expression turned oddly pensive. "You could use some of the estate money to design your own home."

"Nonsense. That would be irresponsible."

"You've made it successful. You deserve some of the benefits."

"The suggestion is absurd."

"The money is there."

"A Montgomery should live at the castle. It's tradition. *God in heaven*. It's called Montgomery Castle."

His brother gave a wobbly smile. Callum seemed...different. Not as jovial, not as rakish, not with that air of nonchalance that Hamish had always found naive. He should be happy that his brother seemed more thoughtful, but instead his demeanor only caused something inside Hamish's chest to ache. *Something is wrong.* The man seemed imbued with a seriousness that seemed entirely uncharacteristic, a seriousness that might come from a preoccupied mind.

Well, whether Callum was pleased or not, Hamish was here to help him. Perhaps money and freedom did not tempt Callum's betrothed, but something would. People were remarkably consistent in succumbing to corruption, no matter the loftiness of their status. Miss Butterworth hadn't seemed like a fool: she should grasp that her position was of the unlofty sort.

A thought occurred to him, and he jerked to a stop. His Hessians squeaked over the marble floor.

Callum swung his gaze toward him. "Hamish?"

"You haven't—er—" Hamish wasn't certain which word to use. The entire thing seemed indelicate.

"What is it?" Callum's voice wobbled. There was that blasted worry again. His brother had never seemed burdened before. He'd always seemed carefree, like some blasted incarnation of Bacchus, just lacking grapes dangling from his hand.

"You don't have an heir on the way?" Hamish asked finally.

His brother widened his eyes. "Nonsense. That would be outrageous."

"It's not outrageous," Hamish said, pondering the physical virtues of Callum's betrothed and his brother's propensity toward impulsiveness.

"Perhaps not," Callum admitted. "But in this case, it's not true. I assure you."

Hamish narrowed his eyes, as if something in his brother's expression might explain what had occurred, and he might discover it if he only scrutinized him sufficiently.

Callum turned around and headed for a staircase. "Follow me."

Hamish did so, noting the wrought iron balusters shaped in the form of scrolls and the glossy banister, which retained the view of the shiny marble foyer. The stairs were of a uniform height, but Hamish had a pang of longing for the stone staircase, the steps worn by age, in Montgomery Castle. What was it that had caused Callum to abandon his life there? And why was he tying his life with someone who would only cause the neighbors anguish?

"You could give some of your work to an estate manager," Callum said.

"That would be far too economically inefficient," Hamish said. "Besides, I do an excellent job."

"Yes," Callum agreed. "But I just want you to have a good time. Time has a habit of passing. I wouldn't want you to have regrets."

"Regrets are only a concern for the illogical who are apt to make poor choices," Hamish said stiffly. "I'm not the person shackling myself to an inappropriate wife."

Callum halted his ascension and he turned to Hamish. His expression was stony. "You mustn't criticize her."

A lesser man would have been intimidated. Hamish fought the strange urge to step back. Callum's firmness and devotion were utterly uncharacteristic.

"She's *English*," Hamish said. "How could I not?"

"She wasn't personally responsible for invading Scotland."

"Well." Hamish huffed. "She benefited from it."

"Our family was hardly decimated. Look at all this." Callum waved his hand in an expansive gesture.

Hamish scowled. "Then tell me this. If there's no heir on the way, is she blackmailing you?"

"Blackmail?"

"You know. Does she have some dreadful information on you? Some crime?"

"Like a murder?" Callum asked uncertainly.

Hamish's eyes widened. "Yes. Like a murder. Though that is an extreme example."

Callum's face was bland.

"You haven't murdered anyone?" Hamish asked, and this time his voice wobbled.

"Me? Of course not."

"You suggested it," Hamish grumbled.

"I can speak in hypothetical terms as well," Callum said. "I had the same tutors, and we attended the same classes."

Hamish tilted his head. "Is her father blackmailing you?"

Fathers could be devious, especially when it came to their daughters. Even Lord McIntyre had been quick to have Callum be betrothed to Lady Isla, and no man exceeded him in virtue.

"Her father is a vicar. No blackmail." This time Callum laughed. It was the first time that evening, and Hamish realized he'd missed the sound.

"That's good," Hamish said, but he kept his voice somber. "But no matter how vile of an act this marriage is, you should know that you can still leave it."

"That's what you came to say?" Callum's eyes still sparkled.

"One of the things," Hamish said, conscious his voice verged on the overly defensive. "I wanted to let you know I am here for you."

"Just don't assume I am marrying a blackmailer."

"Because the fact embarrasses you?" Hamish asked, still suspicious.

"Because it's nonsense. She's composed and dutiful. Sometimes timid. Poor traits for a blackmailer."

"Right." Hamish leaned back and considered his interaction with Callum's fiancée. She'd hardly seemed unassuming, but it would hardly do for him to bring up Miss Butterworth's fiery eyes, her wide grin, and heavens, the feel of her body against his.

His mouth felt dry.

Well. Perhaps there were reasons why Callum *would* want to marry her.

Isla McIntyre might be everything appropriate, but Miss Butterworth was everything inappropriate. There could be pleasure in that.

"I just don't understand," Hamish admitted. "I worked so hard to make certain the estate was earning money again. I studied modern agricultural practices, and it worked. The estate is doing well. Why would you want to lose the castle?"

"Wolfe can have the castle if he wants," Callum said. "Compensation for not marrying his sister."

"But it could be yours. That was the plan."

"Plans change," Callum said. "And I'm not marrying her."

"But there's nothing wrong with Lady Isla," Hamish protested.

"I'm not saying there is," Callum said. "Look. I'm very grateful for your work on the estate. The land is still ours. Just not its—"

"Crown?"

Callum flinched. "It's a castle. Some things are more important."

"It's not just a castle," Hamish protested. "It's our family's history. I could have been studying architecture."

"I'm sorry you couldn't," Callum said.

Hamish averted his eyes.

"Still, you are doing well for yourself," Callum continued.

His brother didn't understand.

Perhaps Hamish had taught himself from books, but he'd never learned from the masters. He'd never been able to truly immerse himself into the world of architecture. He'd always been conscious of the need to keep the estate going.

There had been the war, but Hamish had only joined at the end, when Bonaparte had escaped from Elba, and everything wonderful looked like it might be destroyed after all.

"So you love Miss Butterworth?" The question shouldn't have made Hamish's heart squeeze, and yet it did all the same.

Callum's expression was thoughtful, though he did not answer.

Hamish decided to take the man's silence as a reason to hope. That would suffice until the morning. "If it turns out you don't want to marry her—"

"In that case, I won't," Callum said calmly. "The wedding is the day after tomorrow though."

Hamish gave a miserable nod. "Very well."

"You'll be able to meet Miss Butterworth yourself tomorrow afternoon."

"Perhaps I'll be busy," Hamish said, not really desiring to meet Miss Butterworth with his brother.

"Nonsense," Callum said. "And sadly, they'll want to see you. Her parents are quite pleasant."

Hamish stiffened, and his lips dropped into a frown. They'd had parents and guardians, and had made promises to them that Callum seemed to have no intention of honoring.

Callum led him onto a corridor. It might not be as long as the corridors at Montgomery Castle, but the vases and sideboards scattered in it were of the lavish variety. Finally, Callum opened the door to a large bedroom. Jeweled fabric hung from a canopy bed and lavish curtains draped in a sumptuous manner that signified an inefficient use of fabric. A Persian carpet nearly covered the entire hardwood floor, a similar waste of resources on a room that would be infrequently used. Hamish certainly intended to leave once the wedding was canceled.

"Just promise me," Callum said, "that you won't offend Miss Butterworth or her family during the wedding. I want this to be a joyous occasion for them."

"Very well," Hamish said.

"Oh?" Callum's blue eyes widened, and he smiled.

"Indeed," Hamish said, returning his brother's smile.

I'll ensure she breaks the engagement before the wedding.

Chapter Seven

THE SKY HAD REMAINED dry all night, depriving Georgiana of the satisfaction of envisioning Lord Hamish returning to whatever beastly lair he occupied with muddy clothing.

Georgiana paced her room. Flora had helped her dress, but she was reluctant to go downstairs before she figured out what to do.

Her sister's fiancé had seemed too good to be true. Perfection was something over which to be suspicious.

Well, Georgiana had discovered the man's flaw: his brother was an abomination.

She'd imagined her bridesmaid duties would encompass consultations over hair coiffures and visits to the dressmaker. She'd never imagined it would entail defending her sister's honor late at night from a strange Scotsman.

Men weren't supposed to enter ladies' rooms via balconies. They weren't supposed to enter ladies' rooms at all.

How odd that a man who argued for propriety could behave in a manner so devoid of it.

Men, Georgiana mused, were generally without sense.

A knock sounded on the door. Most likely it was the maid

"Come in," Georgiana called out, while contemplating whether to share news of the encounter with Charlotte. Unfortunately, it was the sort of news that might unnerve even the strongest of spirits, and lovely Charlotte, whatever her merits in pleasantness and overall amiability, could scarcely be called strong. She'd visited too many doctors to be termed that.

The door opened, and her mother strolled into the room.

"M-Mama," Georgiana stammered, conscious her throat had dried some time before her mother reached the *chaise-longue*.

Had someone overheard her last night? Would her mother be demanding a special license and a double wedding? Her mother settled into the velvet chair and pushed the silver candlestick on the side table into its proper position. "My dearest, I have the most delightful news."

"Oh?" Georgiana gave a cautious smile.

"It seems your sister's fiancé's brother arrived last night."

Georgiana forced herself to widen her smile, but a strange feeling in her stomach tossed and turned, as if caught in a stormy sea. Georgiana directed her gaze to the window. The view of the brick townhouse opposite seemed to decidedly belong on land, but her stomach still felt unsettled.

Seeing Lord Hamish did not top her list of desired activities, and yet, curiosity coursed through her.

She wasn't certain she could be in his presence without blushing, her mind returning to last night. Perhaps it was wise to warn her sister of the inadequacies of her future family. Of one thing she was certain: their parents could not know, lest there be an off chance they might desire the funds Lord Hamish offered rather than Charlotte's eternal happiness.

Knowing Mama, she might be happy to declare Georgiana compromised if she learned she'd entertained a midnight visitor, no matter how much Georgiana pleaded the man's visit had been compelled by business, not a romantic urge.

Surely there could be no worse fate than to be saddled to a man of such disagreeableness?

And yet...

Georgiana remembered the feel of his lips pressed against hers, and his scent, that curious mixture of oak and cotton, still seemed to waft over her. His arms might not be holding her, and yet if she closed her eyes, she could sense every contour of his muscles.

The fact was ridiculous. She abhorred rogues.

"I am eager to return to Norfolk," Georgiana said.

Her mother blinked. "You want to accept the curate's offer?"

"Perhaps." She shrugged. "Why not?"

The curate's sensibility was deeply comforting, and for the first time, Georgiana allowed herself to imagine a life with him. It would be lacking any excitement.

Utter bliss.

"We had hoped for better for you, but he does have an agreeable demeanor."

"Why marry at all?"

"That's what I wonder every time I see Mr. Butterworth at breakfast," Mama mused. "He tends to improve by dinnertime, though I'm never certain if it's because of the better attire or because of the dimmer light."

Georgiana contemplated Lord Hamish's offer of a cottage by the sea. That had sounded lovely, and it had almost made her wish she'd been engaged to the duke. Perhaps the more important the bridegroom, the better the bribe to prevent the wedding from occurring.

She descended the stairs with her mother. Her heart thrummed more than was necessary for the activity, girding itself for someone to accuse her of immoral behavior, but everything was much the same as yesterday. Her father and sister joined them on the stairs, but no one mentioned her reputation.

HAMISH PACED THE ROOM. His footsteps were muffled by the thick Persian carpet, and he didn't even have the satisfaction of knowing he was waking Callum. The man should be riddled with guilt. Montgomerys had been living respectably for centuries, all while not succumbing to base desires and joining their name with people who had harmed his family for centuries.

The gold pendulum in the guestroom's clock swung with maddening regularity, even if the polished glass case and well-kept mahogany seemed unlikely harbingers of ill fortune. Yet time *was* running out. The wedding was tomorrow. Had his brother installed the clock to torture him, he would have succeeded.

Still... Where there was a will there was a way, and given the strength of Hamish's will, there must be a myriad of ways in which to break off the engagement. Hamish sat at the desk and tapped his quill on a piece of paper, undistracted by the view of the leafy square. No doubt his brother had not thought he would use the paper to compose ways in which he might shatter Callum's wedding, but then foresight had never been a major asset of his brother's.

The door opened a crack, and a maid appeared. Her eyes widened, perhaps surprised to find him awake, but then she curtsied and moved briskly to the fireplace to light it.

Hamish glanced outside again. Perhaps most people were not awake at dawn, but most people did not have to figure out how to break off a marriage in a day. Most people had no idea of their good fortune.

Hamish wrote *Ways to Stop a Wedding* in large letters over the top of the paper. It was a shame so much attention was spent in how to procure a wedding, rather than how to dissolve it. He was certain many people would be happier without them.

My parents would have been.

He shook his head. No need to ponder them now. They were safely in the ground, enclosed in opulent coffins and blessed with the last rites.

1) Bribery.

This had seemed the cleanest, most expedient solution, providing a more than satisfactory replacement to the inevitable tribulations of marriage, even if Callum's fiancée had not had the good sense to recognize it. He frowned. Evidently, Miss Butterworth desired neither wealth nor independence. *Shame.*

Hamish addressed the maid. "What would cause someone to end an engagement?"

"Well." The maid blinked but gamely pondered the question. She scrunched her lips and twirled a strand of hair. Dabs of coal smeared her fingers, and she dropped the lock. "If she wanted or needed to work, and her workplace didn't allow marriage."

"She doesn't work."

"I suppose if the man drank. Or was a bully. Or if he were with another woman. Or if she weren't fond of the man."

"That's helpful." Hamish nodded encouragingly.

The maid grinned and drew back from the hearth. Orange flames twirled and expanded in size, clambering up the coal and sizzling

"And I suppose she couldn't marry him if there were a problem with the marriage license. But that wouldn't happen, my lord."

He smiled. He had no doubt that Miss Butterworth's family had secured a marriage license. Whatever his brother's faults, he would hardly go to the trouble of setting a wedding date and then not marrying the chit.

Still...

He added the maid's recommendations to the piece of paper.

2) Alcohol

3) Unfaithfulness

4) Hatred

5) License

"You've been helpful," he said. "Miss—er—"

"Eliza." She smiled, curtsied and then hurried from the room.

As the maid's feet pitter-pattered over the corridor, Hamish circled one of the words. An idea spread through his mind, and he contemplated it as the sun rose and the sunbeams that hit the paper grew brighter.

Finally, Hamish stretched his arms. Perhaps Callum was awake. He strode over the corridor and down the stairs, whistling a hunting tune.

The breakfast room was easy to find. Callum was sitting at the long table.

"It's you," his brother said flatly, gesturing toward an empty chair. "I hoped you'd been a figment of my imagination."

"Your imagination isn't capable of conjuring me," Hamish said pleasantly, taking a seat.

"No one's is," Callum murmured.

"I'm sure that's a compliment." Hamish grabbed a roll and dabbed strawberry preserves over it. "I hope you changed your mind about the wedding."

"Nonsense," Callum grumbled.

"And yet you're already awake." Hamish grinned. "At least you were eager to see me."

"I'm eager to visit the club."

Hamish stopped grinning and placed his roll on the blue-and-white china plate. "The day before the wedding? In the morning?"

"I work there."

"You're a duke. You don't have to work."

"And you don't have to be an architect."

"So you take pleasure in belonging to a place of such impropriety?" Hamish asked.

His brother was doing worse than he'd imagined.

Hamish was designing manor houses, but Hamish was certain that managing a club didn't involve anything artistic.

"I'm not doing it by myself," Callum said. "And you really need to be in London more often. It's common knowledge."

"I didn't think you were serious about it."

Callum was silent and poured himself another cup of chocolate.

"Who are you running the club with?" Hamish asked finally.

"Wolfe."

Hamish swallowed hard at the name of their onetime neighbor and the brother of Callum's true betrothed, Lady Isla McIntyre. "What does he think of your intended wedding?"

Callum took a long sip of chocolate, even though, in Hamish's experience, the thick, sweet drink was not conducive to long sips. "He doesn't know."

Hamish raised his eyebrows, and horror must have shown on his face, for his brother sighed.

"He's on holiday," Callum said finally. "He's in Scotland now with his sister, but then he'll sail for France from Liverpool. Apparently, the continent is a place to visit again. Everyone has forgotten Bonaparte."

It was impossible not to note the bitterness in Callum's voice. They'd both fought in the war.

"Bonaparte is being very well guarded at St. Helena," Hamish said finally. "They've learned from their mistakes at Elba. They won't let him escape again, and if he did, he would never be able to raise a strong army. Waterloo was his miracle, and he lost it."

"I don't think France is dangerous," Callum said finally. "But the prospect of returning... I simply couldn't do that. At least not for a holiday."

"I understand."

Architecture allowed Hamish to focus for long periods of time on something completely separate from memories of the war. Designing something new that drew on Scotland's historic traditions, and then concentrating on the small, necessary details to carry it out...that was the closest thing to bliss there was.

"How do you think Wolfe will react?" Hamish asked. Perhaps Wolfe had changed too.

"He'll despise it."

Chapter Eight

FLOWERS AND HERBS FILLED the drawing room. Any books that had once graced the surfaces had been shoved aside, and Georgiana's eyebrows darted up as she entered the room.

Papa seemed similarly flummoxed. "Where is my Plato?"

"Darling!" Mama fluttered her hands. "You don't need Plato! Your daughter is getting married. *Charlotte* is getting married. It's a miracle!"

Charlotte's complexion never ventured far from pale, but it managed to grow lighter now. Georgiana cringed on her behalf. Her mother needn't seem so surprised Charlotte had managed to secure a husband, even though it seemed unlikely a wallflower had somehow captured the match of the season: a duke, one under the age of thirty.

"Nonsense." Papa piled the books back on the parlor table, as if being in such proximity to the titles would convey wisdom. He paused and picked up an herb. "Is that sage on my copy of Plato's *Republic*?"

"Don't move it," Mama exclaimed.

"Is there a particular reason why you have placed sage on it?"

"For our youngest daughter's eternal happiness. It represents wisdom and will go into her bridal bouquet."

"If she believes clutching dried herbs will lead to a life of wisdom, there is no hope for her."

"No doubt you would suggest she stride down the aisle with a philosophy book."

"For instance." Papa stroked his sideburn. "It is always good to ponder the meaning of life."

"Charlotte has already found the meaning of life," her mother said happily. "Marriage."

"Plato would disagree."

"Then he was a foolish man."

"I doubt Plato carried a bridal bouquet of sage on his wedding day," Georgiana said.

"Quite right," Mama said. "He probably should have done that. Though a boutonniere of course. Far more masculine."

"Plato wore a toga," Papa grumbled. "He couldn't possibly have worn a boutonniere."

"You don't know that," Mama said merrily, concentrating on arranging the herbs. "Just because the statues don't show boutonnieres, doesn't mean men didn't wear them."

"Mother has a good point," Georgiana said, and her mother smiled triumphantly.

"Besides, he never married," Papa said.

"You are simply proving my point, dear," Mama declared.

"Hmph." Papa continued to scrutinize the room. "Please tell me that isn't garlic."

"Would you desire our child to be without goodness?" Mama asked.

"The garlic will ward off any invitations for misbehaving." Papa turned to Charlotte. "I'm no proponent of misbehaving, but do you really want garlic in your bridal bouquet?"

"If Mama desires it," Charlotte said. "It does not matter."

Georgiana frowned. Charlotte had been surprisingly nonchalant about the whole wedding. It was almost as if she were not madly in love with the duke, and if she were not in love with him, perhaps he was not in love with her.

Despite her fondness for her sister, even Georgiana had to admit the strangeness of their match. Their mother would have considered it a victory if Charlotte had merely danced with the duke, an occurrence to bring up on dull, cold nights in Norfolk, but instead Charlotte had appeared with a Scottish heirloom on her finger and the duke's vow to be permanently at her side.

"I always thought Georgiana would marry first," Mama said.

"Because she's the oldest?" Papa settled into an armchair, apparently satisfied to have discovered his copy of *The Republic* and leafed through the pages, occasionally brushing away strands of dried herbs.

"Because her thighs are the largest and more conducive to birthing," Mama said, obviously unaware she'd managed to insult both her children at the same time.

Their mother was wrong. Charlotte was pretty, though it wouldn't matter if she wasn't.

Georgiana's sister had always been thin, perhaps because she'd always been sickly. She'd retreated into the world of books and music, barricaded in the family's drawing room.

Until she'd become engaged.

Before Georgiana.

Georgiana was happy for her sister. Truly she was. Still, Georgiana had the impression Charlotte was refraining from sharing everything with her, and she did not exactly delight in the raised eyebrows by some in the *ton*. They thought it odd Georgiana, who was in her third season, had managed to be bested by someone who was in her first season. Since Georgiana was supposed to have all the advantages of health, they seemed to delight in pondering what disadvantages in personality she possessed.

She sighed. In two days, her sister would be married and whisked off to some castle in Scotland, and Georgiana would remain in London.

Georgiana busied herself with some crocheting. The task was hampered by visions of broad shoulders and large green eyes. Her late night visitor's Scottish brogue seemed to continue to whisper into her ear.

Voices sounded from the entry, but this time Georgiana was less confident than normal. She smoothed her dress, though an unbecoming wrinkle was not her chief worry.

The duke's younger brother had attempted to bribe her in an effort to prevent the wedding from occurring and then had insulted her morals by kissing her. She seethed.

There was still time to confess everything to her family. She could leap to her feet and lock the door or at least drag one of the heavier chairs to block the entrance, since she'd never actually seen a key for the door.

Papa might chase the duke's brother from the house, as was entirely appropriate. But would he chase the duke away as well, believing the lack of character in the man's younger brother indicated a lack of character in the duke?

Georgiana wasn't certain, and she had the dreadful idea Mama might be happy to shout "compromised" if she learned her daughter had been alone with a man who was under the age of thirty-five and resided in a castle. And dear Charlotte, what if she put an end to the wedding, after feeling herself unwelcome in the Montgomery family?

No, it was better for Georgiana to remain silent and to only discuss weather if asked to converse. She gave a quick glance to the window. The sky was gray, and it drizzled outside.

Good.

She could work with that. She could say, "When will the rain ever stop?" and "I much prefer sunshine to drizzle."

"My son!" Mama called out, leaping from her seat in a manner not precisely advocated by etiquette books. "Here he is, with his dearest brother."

"Are you certain?" Georgiana asked, aware too late her voice had somehow managed to become hoarse. She coughed.

Her mother turned her head toward her. "Please tell me you're not becoming ill."

"N-No." Georgiana shook her head with vigor, but the increased rapidity did not lessen the narrowing of Mama's eyes.

"Are you quite all right, dear?" Mama placed her right palm over Georgiana's forehead.

Evidently Georgiana was not as successful at feigning confidence as she'd hoped.

Fiddle-faddle.

"I'm perfectly well, Mama." Georgiana forced herself to smile, but even though lip moving was a skill she was certain she'd mastered, her attempt must have contained a wobble, for her mother continued to scrutinize her.

Footsteps struck against the corridor, unhampered by the carpets. The noise was the sort that could only be achieved by muscular men wearing Hessians.

It will be fine. It will be fine. It will be fine.

At least the duke's brother had decided to make a more conventional entrance this time.

It would be quite nice to slink up to her room and avoid him, but who knew what the man might say to Charlotte? No, she would remain here. At least she could glower at him if he approached her sister. Her lips twitched. And perhaps he would stay away from them both if he thought she did have some contagious disease from a faraway land that would flummox any doctor or surgeon.

"Your health is vital," Mama said. "What if you were to make the duke ill? What if he could never marry dear Charlotte? Why, you could have typhoid. Malaria!"

"I don't have typhoid or malaria," Georgiana said, managing to step away from her mother's enthusiastic attempts at medical administrations. "How could I have caught them here?"

"This isn't Norfolk," her mother said. "There are a number of ships from all sorts of foreign places sitting in the Thames. They could be filled with all sorts of deadly diseases." Her mother leaned closer. "Some not even identified. You could be the first case on English soil."

"I feel fine," Georgiana said hastily.

Her mother looked almost disappointed, as if the prospect of being the mother to the first Englishwoman to succumb to a newly discovered tropical illness appealed to her imagination.

"Are you well, Miss Butterworth?" The faint Scottish brogue of her sister's fiancé sounded. It was concerned and proper, but Georgiana's heartrate still quickened.

If the duke was here, his brother was most likely also present.

Even though Georgiana had decided she despised the man from the moment he'd invaded her chamber, the memory of his lips on hers still managed to be pleasant.

Would he announce that he knew her already?

Naturally not.

He wasn't a fool. If he didn't want his brother to marry dear sweet lovely Charlotte, who had all the advantages of temperament, he wouldn't want to go about announcing he'd compromised her sister.

Georgiana glided her gaze to the entrance. The duke managed to look as handsome as ever, but his arrogant brother was beside him.

How odd two men who resembled each other in appearance could so drastically differ in temperament. Though his hair was darker than his brother's, their shoulders were of similar widths, and their legs were of similar lengths. Their noses did not differ in the steepness of their slopes, and their chins were both of the wide variety.

"I'm quite fine." Georgiana drew back, unsure what precisely he might say, and not caring to inspire him to action.

"It looked like you were ill," the duke's brother said, his voice cool.

"Er—no." She flushed. She should be prepared for the man's lilting, sonorous voice, but it only reminded her of last night's kiss.

"I thought the same thing. But now I believe she was only overwhelmed at the prospect of meeting you," Mama said, utterly unhelpfully. "Such excitement for my poor child. You must be the dear duke's brother."

"Yes."

"It's a pleasure to meet you." Her mother dipped into a low curtsy. "Your brother has told us so much about you. An architect!"

"My specialty is in the Scots baronial style."

"How fascinating." Mama fixed a bland smile on her face, the kind she wore when she was utterly bemused, but thought a smile appropriate. "History is important."

"Indeed. I think it vital people not forget the cruelty of the English in past interactions with the Scottish."

An awkward silence followed, and then her mother laughed. "You are really too charming."

The duke's brother's face did not change. "History is no comedy."

"Er—quite right," Papa said. "Would you like some tea?"

Georgiana smiled. Papa had never been an enthusiastic tea drinker before, but he seemed eager to have something with which to distract himself. He soon launched into a soliloquy on the types of tea, one which did not seem to intrigue the duke's brother, no doubt because it did not involve trespassing.

"It is a pleasure to finally meet my brother's betrothed." Lord Hamish directed his gaze in Georgiana's direction.

Georgiana shifted on the sofa. The pillows were soft, but not soft enough to ease the tension in her body.

This was when she was going to be discovered.

This was when he would discover she was not in fact her sister, and that she'd had no business speaking with authority on the betrothal.

"Dear child, you look so pale," Mama said abruptly.

"Perhaps you require more tea," Lord Hamish said. "Apparently it has a great many restorative powers."

Papa clapped his hands together. "Oh, indeed. We could even bring out the green variety."

"I'm quite fine," she said weakly.

Tea was expensive. It was a delicacy appropriate to serve to a duke and his brother, but she could hardly have two cups of it.

Her parents had intended that the family would leave London earlier, when it was evident Georgiana had yet again not acquired a fiancé, but her sister's unexpected betrothal had changed that. Georgiana would be glad when her sister married, and they could return to Norfolk and its pleasant countryside, away from the grime of the capital.

Chapter Nine

THE DRAWING ROOM WAS small and covered with books and flowers.

They were all there together: Callum, Miss Butterworth, her two parents and a sister.

Not that Miss Butterworth seemed particularly lively now. She seemed to be doing her best to imitate a shrinking wallflower.

He smirked. She could never disappear into the scenery. Her eyes were far too expressive, and that hair was far too red.

Her sister was more successful at being nondescript, and he noted pale hair, a willowy figure, and a bottle green dress that did not benefit her complexion. Still...her gaze felt intelligent, and from time to time he felt her gaze on him.

His lips twitched. In truth, there was no need for either sibling to speak. Their mother seemed determined to hold a conversation for everyone. She spoke rapidly, her eyes glimmering and her lips turning into such a large smile, Hamish almost felt guilty.

No matter.

His brother had given only the most cursory greeting to Miss Butterworth, and the woman did appear most nervous.

Hamish might never have contemplated marriage, much less a love match, but he knew that it should consist of more than cursory greetings. He smirked and turned to Miss Butterworth. "My brother has not told me much about you."

She stiffened.

"But why would he?" Mrs. Butterworth asked, inexplicably rising to Callum's defense.

A pink flush spread over Miss Butterworth's cheeks, and she smoothed her dress. She needn't. It looked fine, if a trifle shabby.

Hamish glanced at his brother, who was occupied in sipping tea and staring out of the room's single window. Though Hamish was fond of views as well, this one seemed underwhelming when compared to protecting one's betrothed's sensibilities. *God in heaven.* Perhaps Callum was preoccupied, but he'd got himself into this mess. The man had seemed melancholic all day, and his brother always exuded sanguinity.

Perhaps Callum did not want to irritate his future mother-in-law. It was not as if they had another mother, and even Lady McIntyre had passed away.

Hamish's chest squeezed, and he turned to Mrs. Butterworth. "I would have thought you would have imagined he'd told me something about her."

"Nonsense." Mrs. Butterworth shook her head with such vigor that the lace trimmings on her cap whipped about, while keeping an entirely inappropriate smile on her face. "You've just reunited with your brother again. I expect you've had other things to discuss."

"Well," Hamish said, recognizing some logic in her words. "That is true."

"Of course it is." Mrs. Butterworth beamed. "I would much rather hear about the castle. The dear duke said you actually live in it."

Hamish adjusted the positioning of his pillow. The armchair seemed devoid of any comfort, and the pillows did not provide any improvement.

"I do live in a castle." Hamish glanced at his brother, but Callum was feigning great enthusiasm at a leather tome. "For *now*."

"How very delightful. It's too delightful for words," Mrs. Butterworth exclaimed.

"And yet you've been able to add many words," Mr. Butterworth remarked.

Mrs. Butterworth blushed. "Perhaps. Oh, but I am thrilled about this whole marriage."

Her eyes glimmered again, and Hamish turned away, conscious of that strange feeling of guilt again. Now was not the time for his tutors' pontifications on ethics to finally affect him. Besides, who knew how many generations of future Montgomerys he was assisting?

"Tell me about your first meeting with my brother," he asked Miss Butterworth.

"Oh, but I can tell the story!" Mrs. Butterworth cried out.

Miss Butterworth swallowed hard. This was a woman who'd comfortably brandished a candlestick before him. Why was she unsettled now?

"It's really not necessary, Mama," Miss Butterworth said.

"I'm happy to tell it." Mrs. Butterworth leaned forward, and some pillows toppled from behind her. "I witnessed the whole thing."

"Indeed," Hamish said.

"From this very chair!" Mrs. Butterworth exclaimed, and Hamish scrunched his eyebrows together.

"You mean my brother just called on this household?"

Mrs. Butterworth nodded eagerly. "Yes. That's how he met my dear daughter. Just like that."

"That's most unusual," Hamish said.

"You think so?" Mrs. Butterworth widened her eyes. "I thought it was actually pedestrian."

"You see? None of your stories are pedestrian, my dear." Mr. Butterworth's face glowed, despite the sideburns that valiantly covered a large portion. "I've been trying to tell her that for years."

Mrs. Butterworth laughed. "He just wants to stay in Norfolk."

Hamish's brows remained furrowed, and he set his now empty teacup on the table, wedging it between two stacks of books. "But how did my brother know to call at precisely this household?"

It felt incredibly wrong.

Except... He could believe the Butterworths and his brother were not in the same circles. Mr. Butterworth was a vicar, and Callum—well, Callum was a duke who apparently devoted his time to a gaming club.

Mrs. Butterworth stretched and refilled Hamish's teacup with the casual expertise of a woman accustomed to being surrounded by books and undaunted by the fear of tipping a tower over or submerging a tome in hot liquid. "I suppose he must have asked my other daughter. I never inquired."

"I find that a most intriguing question." Hamish tapped his fingers over his armrest, vaguely noting that Miss Butterworth seemed to be slinking into the sofa.

Mrs. Butterworth clapped her hands, and her curls bounced, unhampered by her white cap, generously laden with ribbons. "Do you know? I think you just might have a point."

"And then when did they become engaged?" Hamish asked.

"Oh, by the end of the afternoon, I believe."

"How very expedient." Hamish glanced at his brother, who seemed to be taking an interest in the floral bouquets and did not meet his eyes.

On another occasion Hamish may have laughed. Callum had never found flower arrangements of much interest before.

"My daughter *is* very beautiful," Mrs. Butterworth said, taking another sip of tea. "Most angelic."

Hamish's lips twitched. Angelic was not the word he would select to describe Miss Butterworth. He doubted Mrs. Butterworth would appreciate his opinion on that particular matter and he turned to his brother. "But why did you propose with such haste?"

"It—er—" Callum seemed for once at a loss for words.

Hamish frowned. The man's behavior was most unconventional, but the mild-mannered Mr. Butterworth did not seem to be a blackmailer.

"Obviously it was love at first sight. Or nearly first sight." Mrs. Butterworth's voice wobbled somewhat. No doubt she'd also been surprised by Miss Butterworth's hasty engagement to the duke.

"More tea?" the other Miss Butterworth asked.

It was the first thing she'd said.

"Splendid idea." Callum smiled and gallantly helped her.

Hamish scrunched his eyebrows and struggled to recollect if Callum had ever helped with tea before.

"When will the rain ever stop?" Miss Butterworth asked abruptly.

Everyone appeared puzzled. The conversation halted, and Callum reclined in his seat. Hamish was again struck by the room's small size. He heard the sound of feet sliding over the floorboards as people readjusted their positions and teacups clanging on saucers, but not the patter of raindrops.

"Well, it's hardly affecting us indoors," Mrs. Butterworth said finally.

"I merely wondered—"

"I believe it's stopped now," Hamish said.

Miss Butterworth looked to the window, no doubt discovering the sky was of the clear variety. Her cheeks pinkened.

The room was silent, *more* awkward than before.

"I much prefer sunshine to drizzle," Miss Butterworth said.

"For the sake of the flowers?" Callum smiled. "My dear brother. Did you know Miss Butterworth is quite interested in garden design? I believe you might find you have some things in common. My brother is of course an architect."

"I was unaware," Hamish said, assessing Miss Butterworth.

Garden design. That was intriguing. Not of course as intriguing as architecture, but what else was?

"She redesigned our garden at home three times," Mr. Butterworth said, his voice brimming with fatherly pride. "Every summer a new design. I think she wants me to become a deacon just so she has a larger garden to work with."

Some expression changed on Mrs. Butterworth's face, and she gestured toward her daughter. "Do you not find her pretty as well, Lord Hamish?"

"Er—quite pretty," Hamish said, conscious his voice felt hoarse, and not daring to look in Callum's direction. *Well.* He could hardly say that his brother's betrothed was *not* pretty.

Unfortunately contemplating her physical features made him remember exploring those same physical features last night, and that was not something he should be doing in the parlor, with her parents, sister, and fiancé in the room.

"I do hope you will remain in London. You must dance with her. The waltz. It's more romantic."

Hamish blinked.

"Romantic dances are always the best sort." Mrs. Butterworth nodded, as if she'd simply declared a preference for a particular park.

"I doubt the waltz would be appropriate," Hamish said. "Perhaps we could attempt a cotillion?"

"Do you not waltz, my lord? Perhaps Mr. Butterworth might give you lessons. I have found him an excellent waltzer."

The two exchanged such affectionate glances that something in Hamish's heart panged. The room might be small, and no fire blazed in the hearth, but the atmosphere exuded warmth.

"I waltz," Hamish admitted.

"Splendid." Mrs. Butterworth clapped with such vigor that she seemed to bounce on the sofa cushions. "Then it's settled."

Miss Butterworth's face paled.

"I mean, she is going to be my brother's wife," Hamish said. "I thought a cotillion might be considered more appropriate."

Too late it occurred to him that keeping Miss Butterworth from dancing excessively romantic dances with his brother might be in Hamish's best interest.

"Oh, no." Mrs. Butterworth shook her head adamantly. "Miss *Charlotte* Butterworth is to be your new sister."

"I did not have an old one," Hamish grumbled.

"Even more splendid! But what I mean is that your brother is not planning to marry my older, auburn-haired Georgiana."

And then he understood.

He'd attempted to bribe the wrong sister.

No wonder she'd refused to be swayed.

"You mean—" Hamish's Adam's apple somersaulted.

"Are you sure you're quite well?" Callum placed a floral bouquet back on the table, and his voice was filled with such brotherly concern Hamish had the unfortunate realization that his shock must be blatantly evident.

"I'm fine," Hamish said, though his voice sounded of the strangled variety. "I'm just surprised."

Callum frowned. "But why would you think I was marrying *her*?"

Georgiana's face pinkened, and outrage shot through Hamish's body. There was nothing wrong with Georgiana. She'd make an excellent duchess, even if he had spent last night attempting to convince her of the contrary.

He glanced at the other Miss Butterworth. *Charlotte.* She was blonde, slim. He should have guessed she would be Callum's choice.

And yet, having met Georgiana, he'd never once considered that his brother would marry the other sister.

"Dear Lord Hamish," Miss Charlotte Butterworth said, taking charge of the conversation. "How was your travel from Scotland? I trust the weather was tolerable?"

"The state of the sky does not impede on my enjoyment of things."

"He never enjoys things," Callum said, and the others laughed.

Hamish glowered. They shouldn't laugh. Laughing was uncalled for.

He'd tried to bribe the wrong woman.

And worse, he'd kissed her.

Well. It might be difficult to ascribe the kiss as being too horrible. So far in London the kiss had been by far his best experience, though he could hardly admit that to the others who seemed determined to make pleasant conversation with him, as if such a thing could ever be possible after having discovered that his brother was ruining his life and that of future Montgomerys.

Hamish gazed at the red-headed Butterworth and then averted his eyes away quickly, lest her mother, obviously in matchmaking mode, decided to expound more on the loveliness of her eldest daughter and the vast pleasure he would experience by repeating the steps of some dreadful continental dance with her.

Not that there might not be *some* pleasure in waltzing with her. Something about holding one hand on her waist and clasping her hand was not dreadful to contemplate, though in all likelihood, knowing her, she might be prone to grip his hand in an attempt to discern whether she might shatter it and to wear some form of hair belt around her waist to cause him discomfort.

At least it was less dreadful than the rest of the activities in London. He supposed he should be thankful no one had suggested they go shopping at the Bond Street Bazaar for wedding attire.

Still.

The lassie could have told him. It was dashed embarrassing to have made a whole speech to the wrong woman. He'd been proud of his phrasing and in all likelihood, he wouldn't be able to repeat it to the same effect. It was difficult to make an impassioned speech to someone after spending the afternoon discussing varieties of teas.

Besides, how would he even access Miss Charlotte Butterworth's chamber? He could hardly go about traipsing the corridors of the Butterworths' townhouse, no matter how politely they might converse about the weather. A house like this was bound to have more than one candlestick.

So far his attempt at stopping the wedding was not going well. He would need to contemplate other means. He scrutinized the room, and something in his gaze must have made his brother wary.

Callum placed his teacup on the table. "We'll not stay long."

"Naturally," Mrs. Butterworth said. "I expect you will want to prepare for tomorrow's wedding."

Hamish thought quickly. He couldn't leave just yet. He needed to make some progress. He needed to spend less time focusing on Miss Georgiana Butterworth and more time in making Miss Charlotte Butterworth reconsider her hasty attachment.

There seemed to be hope. This was evidently a whirlwind romance, and any fool knew whirlwinds never ended well.

He mused over the words of Callum's maid, who'd possessed the supremely sensible name of Eliza, one that did not evoke half-dressed figures from antiquity.

She'd noted alcohol, unfaithfulness and dislike for the groom as deterrents to marriage. Naturally dislike could be disregarded. There was nothing about Callum to dislike. The man was a Montgomery, after all. Unfortunately, Hamish could hardly find another woman in the drawing room to say Callum had dallied with her.

But alcohol... He could do something about that. Hamish would be a fool to not take advantage of the fact they were drinking.

"I would like to try the green tea," Hamish said.

Mr. Butterworth beamed. "Splendid. I was worried you might find it to be too strong."

"Nonsense," Hamish said. "I like a hearty taste."

"You should see him eat black pudding," Callum said.

"Well then." Mr. Butterworth's eyes glimmered. "You'll probably like it more than I do."

Hamish grinned. He'd brought a flask of alcohol with him. The very strongest sort. It would be easy to slip some of the drink into his brother's cup. Callum was likely so inexperienced with green tea he wouldn't even realize that the strong, delicious flavor was not supposed to be there.

Soon they were given the tea.

Hamish stretched and doused Callum's tea with a heavy dose of special Scottish whisky, thankful for the towers of books. He strove to not smile when Callum raised the teacup to his lips.

"How do you like it?" Mr. Butterworth inquired.

"I enjoy it very much," Hamish said.

"The man does seem pleased," Mrs. Butterworth said merrily. "I do believe he enjoys the tea. Who knew a man would appreciate the bitter taste so much?"

"Oh, it's much less bitter than I expected." Callum downed his teacup with a rapidity not associated with the drink.

Hamish leaned back into his armchair. In no time Callum would act rather less polished than was his tendency.

Chapter Ten

THE DUKE SEEMED TO be swaying, and Georgiana narrowed her eyes. His face was flushed, and the strands of his blond hair lay flat against his forehead, darkened in color as if he were battling a fever.

Or something more nefarious.

One didn't live in less than fashionable areas and not see someone drunk. The singing that graced the streets on the edges of Mayfair were never of the proper sort, sung by trained opera singers who'd had each note assessed by plump Italian masters who viewed the accomplishment of each note as a greater feat than any show of athletic prowess.

The singing in Norfolk seemed confined to sailor ditties, whether sung by actual sailors, refined men who were in their less sober moments still enthusiastic about their days at sea, or those who simply had romantic urges toward piracy, best expressed in counting imaginary rum bottles and the merits of Spanish ladies.

The duke was not singing, but he *had* begun to whistle, and though he might be trying to impress Charlotte with his ability to carry a tune, it was not something he'd done before.

The duke was also not known to stumble, but his eyes were narrowed, as if concentrating to reach the door, an exploit no doubt made more difficult by his sudden inclination to sway.

Papa shut his book, and his bland expression firmed. "Are you quite alright, Your Grace?"

"Yeth." The duke waved his hand with such force he nearly tipped over. "A walking stick would be nice." He turned to his brother, and his gaze developed a dreamy aura to which she was not accustomed. "Remember when we used to carve walking sticks from branches in the woods?"

"Ah." Lord Hamish gave a condescending smile. "That's a sign of your great imagination."

"That ith not true." The duke's face reddened.

"My brother is quite prone to fantasy," Lord Hamish said conversationally.

"He also seems prone to drink," Papa said.

"Mr. Butterworth!" Mama gave an outraged sigh. "What exactly are you implying?"

"Just that," Papa said. "He's an imbiber. A topper. A—"

"He must have become inebriated," the duke's brother said. "I do apologize. It only happens when he is most bored."

There was a silence.

"He must have had a flask," Lord Hamish said. "It is so very kind of your daughter to marry my brother."

"Kind?" Papa's eyes widened predictably, and Georgiana's heart tumbled. No doubt Lord Hamish was trying to besmirch the duke.

Lord Hamish nodded. "Yes. Kind, given my brother's propensity to alcohol."

The silence continued, and Georgiana shifted her legs, contemplating whether she could contradict the duke's brother.

"He's no such thing. Our new son is sober and dutiful," Mama said.

"He's not your new son yet," Lord Hamish reminded her parents.

"Perhaps His Grace is not my new son yet in a strict mathematical sense," Mama conceded, "Though when one applies the law of averages..."

"How very true," Lord Hamish said. "How kind you are here given my brother's propensity toward distemper."

"Violence?" Mama's eyes widened.

The duke's brother's face reddened, and he did not meet Georgiana's eyes. "Well. Er—not precisely violence. But he knows how to grumble."

"Ah, but so do I," Mama said, her voice once again merry. "She'll be quite at home, I'm certain." Mama turned to Georgiana's father. "Did you hear that, dear? My new son likes to grumble too! And you said I did it with too much frequency. But now it will help dear Charlotte's marriage!"

"Good," Papa murmured with the dispassion of a man who knew just which word to say.

"I want a walking stick," the duke drawled from the settee.

"Mr. Butterworth, fetch the poor man a walking stick," Mama ordered.

"But I haven't got one," he protested. "The pavement in London does not require it."

"Our son is in pain, and you are spending the time boasting about your ambling abilities?" Mama's face was stern, and Papa's face crumpled.

"I didn't mean—"

"Of course you didn't mean," Mama said. "You never mean, despite all the time thinking you do with those supposedly great philosophers to help you."

Papa's face reddened. "Perhaps a servant will have one."

The servants were not in possession of a walking stick. Apparently they were also adept at walking, a fact that no doubt helped them maintain their positions, and none of them were in the habit of mirroring Beau Brummel's expensive yet stark dress sense and were in possession of canes.

"How unfortunate my brother is in an inappropriate state," Lord Hamish said with such innocence Georgiana frowned.

Perhaps he was the brother of a duke, and perhaps she should attempt to act less impulsively, but Lord Hamish couldn't allow her parents and sister to have any unwarranted doubts about the duke.

"Are you by any chance referring to the fact you put a strange substance in your brother's drink?" Georgiana asked.

Lord Hamish widened his eyes, and she gave him her sweetest smile.

"Is that true, my lord?" Papa asked, managing to convey both sternness and confusion.

Lord Hamish's face whitened. Perhaps he was reminded of the fact that Papa was a vicar and had given morals great consideration.

"I do not approve," Papa said, managing to convey such authority that Georgiana almost felt sorry for Lord Hamish. Papa might be hoary-haired, but he could intimidate.

"Sibling teasing," Georgiana suggested. "Am I correct?"

"Er—yes." Lord Hamish guided his brother from the room, making use of his sturdy arms which Georgiana wished she were not quite so aware of.

Chapter Eleven

LONDON COULD NOT BE relied upon to have nice weather, even in the midst of spring and even on important wedding days. So much of Georgiana's time in London had been spent ducking under awnings and porticos when sudden onslaughts of rain had hampered the daily stroll she shared with her mother and sister. The occasional evening ball and a townhouse they couldn't quite afford seemed poor compensation for the cozy vicarage they'd abandoned. This day, though, was different.

Sunbeams danced on every surface, illuminating buildings and branches with indiscretion. Once dour squares radiated magnificence, and even the Londoners smiled. The opulent coach, a castoff from Georgiana's grandfather and splendid in a manner only achieved by people in the last century, rattled over the cobblestones.

Everyone wore their finest attire. Mama had managed to get Papa to try a more advanced cravat knot, and she'd selected a turban of such magnificence she had to duck her head to best ensure the feathers' continued beauty.

Georgiana smoothed the netting of her new canary-colored gown. Cheerful ribbons trimmed the hem. It was the finest dress Georgiana had ever owned.

"That dress is the most impractical thing I've ever seen," Papa remarked. "That gauze can tear easily."

"It's fashionable," Mama exclaimed.

"Only so women will need to see their dressmaker quickly again. Even the color is too light and susceptible to stains."

"Georgiana will not eat anything until the wedding breakfast," Mama said. "By which time her sister will be a duchess. Besides, she might always remain your little girl, but she is quite capable of getting through the wedding without the destruction of her attire."

"Thank you, Mama," Georgiana said.

"And after Charlotte marries her duke, you can marry the duke's brother. It will make holidays so convenient."

Just as quickly Georgiana's spirits fell. "The man was attempting to make his brother drunk."

"Attempting?" Papa snorted. "He succeeded."

"Success is a virtue," Mama declared.

"Not that sort," Georgiana said hastily, hoping to convey satisfactory indignation without conveying that Charlotte's future brother-in-law was utterly despicable.

"Besides, you noticed his action, my dear," Mama said. "There seemed a definite spark between you."

On that Georgiana could somewhat agree, though she refrained from remarking that any spark derived from Lucifer, a person Lord Hamish undoubtedly would find himself spending very much time with in the afterlife.

The coach slowed and rattled over the cobblestones, and the elegant columns of St. George's portico came into view. Georgiana and Charlotte leaned toward the window. Charlotte's veil fluttered with the additional movement, and her face remained somber.

A trickle of uncertainty moved through Georgiana at her sister's expression, but Charlotte had a habit of being serious, and marriage must have its serious aspects.

"Sit down, Charlotte. You'll crease your dress," Mama said. "You wouldn't want the dear duke to think you prone to gallivanting about in wrinkles. He would question your housekeeping abilities."

"The duke will not be depending on her for housekeeping abilities," Papa said. "She's going to be a duchess."

"Well, she'll have to tell servants if she sees wrinkles so they can correct it," Mama said, though it seemed obvious she'd only said that to be correct.

Finally, the coach halted.

"Mr. Butterworth and I will greet the minister," Mama said. "Wait five minutes, girls. We need to make sure the duke is not at the entrance. He mustn't see dear Charlotte before the wedding ceremony begins. Who knows what might happen?"

"That is really no concern, Mrs. Butterworth," Papa said. "If the man had changed his mind, we would not be here."

Their parents left, still arguing amiably, and Georgiana was left alone with her sister.

This was the last time she'd be alone with Charlotte before she married. They'd been alone hours upon hours before this, but these minutes felt monumental.

"I'm so very happy for you," Georgiana said.

"Thank you." The words were appropriate, but Georgiana wondered whether Charlotte's eyes should sparkle more. Instead, her fingers trembled, a less reassuring action.

Despite Georgiana's unmarried state, she imagined some nervousness would be normal.

"I'm certain the duke will take excellent care of you," Georgiana said, using her most reassuring voice.

"He has been most agreeable."

Agreeable wasn't precisely the word Georgiana would select to describe a future husband, but then, despite their shared proclivity for romantic stories, Charlotte was perhaps too timid to pontificate on her betrothed's qualities like some Shakespearean heroine tasked with a soliloquy.

"I hope you'll be very happy," Georgiana said, certain she should be offering some words of wisdom, but aware she had none. She opened the carriage door and descended the steps, waiting for Charlotte to do the same. "And don't mind the man's brother."

"Lord Hamish?" Humor emanated through Charlotte's voice. "Why on earth are you thinking of him?"

"I found him...unpleasant." Georgiana tossed her hair, though she soon regretted the action. Sudden sharp movements were unlikely to benefit her updo.

Charlotte nodded, but her eyebrows seemed to have ascended to a placement a trifle higher than was their natural perch.

Hmph. Georgiana's cheeks were definitely warmer than they had been previously. In fact, even the back of her neck seemed to have risen several degrees, as if they'd driven into Cairo, and not merely Hanover Square.

Georgiana should refrain from further babbling. Charlotte didn't need to spend the last moments of her unmarried life listening to criticisms of her ever-impending brother-in-law.

After all, the marriage was happening.

They were here, and Charlotte looked magnificent in her very best gown. The ivory color suited her.

"You look beautiful. Let's go to the church." Georgiana helped her sister from the coach. She adjusted Charlotte's veil and floral crown and then gave Charlotte her bouquet.

They strode toward the building. The elaborate portico and columns gleamed under the bright light. Curious onlookers smiled at them, no doubt recognizing that Charlotte was a bride.

"And now for the start of the rest of your life," Georgiana murmured.

Charlotte gave her a soft smile, but the sides of her eyes didn't crinkle, and Georgiana wondered again whether there was any chance Lord Hamish might be correct after all. Had Charlotte forced the duke to marry her? Were they not bonded by love?

The thought was obviously impossible.

Georgiana followed Charlotte up the steps to the church. No music wafted from the inside, but birds chirped merrily.

All the same Georgiana's heartbeat had decided to quicken, sending blood through her body at a normally unnecessary pace. Perhaps she should say...something. "You don't have to marry him."

Charlotte's face wobbled, but then she smiled. "Naturally."

They embraced, and a few of the people outside clapped.

"Come, let's enter before the duke and his brother arrive. We can speak to the minister." Georgiana placed her hand on the door handle and pushed.

The door didn't budge, and she pushed again.

And again.

"I'll try it." Charlotte brushed her veil from her face, and blonde wisps of hair spilled over her forehead as she strove to open the door.

This wasn't how Charlotte's wedding was supposed to go.

"Perhaps there is a different entrance," Georgiana said hopefully.

The statement seemed an absurd one. What other entrance could the minister have intended them to use?

Georgiana glanced at the onlookers. "This is where the brides normally enter?"

The onlookers nodded, appearing puzzled, and her heart sank.

THE COACH JOSTLED ON the way to the chapel, and Hamish whistled. Perhaps yesterday morning had not gone well, but fortunately his list had included multiple methods of wedding deterrence. He attempted a complex melody, hitting each note exquisitely.

His brother widened his eyes and removed his glossy hat. "Are you happy?"

"Perhaps," Hamish said nonchalantly.

"On my wedding day?"

"Aye."

"Good," Callum said with a skeptical tone that was entirely deserved. He ran his fingers along the brim of his top hat, then adjusted his boutonniere. He exuded nervous energy.

"Those flowers are most flamboyant."

"It's a special occasion," Callum grumbled. "Not a regular occurrence."

"I hope not," Hamish said. "I don't like being dragged to London. The ride is unpleasant."

"England is beautiful."

"Not in—"

"Comparison with Scotland. I know. You've—er—mentioned it. I suppose you'll be back soon enough." Callum glanced at Hamish's trunk.

Hamish flushed. Perhaps it had been forward of him to travel with his trunk, but he abhorred the thought of remaining in London. Remaining in London might cause him to call on Miss Georgiana Butterworth, and that would be dreadful. He would be able to catch a stagecoach in Smithfield Market and be rid of this town.

"It would do you well to remember Scotland," Hamish huffed, "given your position as one of Scotland's premiere nobles."

Callum gave a tight smile.

"You could still change your mind," Hamish said.

"I know."

Hamish raised his eyebrows.

"I mean, obviously it's a possibility. That's just common sense," Callum said. "We're not yet linked to each other."

"For all eternity."

Callum shifted his legs. His expression seemed to grow more serious, and he moved his head toward the window.

If Callum flinched when Hamish described the wedding as lasting for all eternity, well, that was a sign the marriage shouldn't be happening.

People married for duty all the time, especially when their names came with fancy titles, but they did not marry virtual commoners. Was his brother madly in love with Miss Charlotte Butterworth? It was a question that should have been meaningless. Weren't romances confined to penny dreadfuls that were essentially fairy tales? Marriages were legal contacts vital to the functioning of society. Perhaps at times love was involved, but that was not a necessary ingredient in a successful marriage. Still, some romance-filled people might revolt against his realism, but surely that only pertained to cases in which love existed.

Hamish smiled and stretched nonchalantly. The guilt that had accompanied him from Scotland dissipated, and he relaxed against the sumptuous pillows.

Callum looked at him curiously, as if he were expecting Hamish to make another protest, but Hamish refrained from doing so.

It would all be over soon.

The Butterworths must already be at the chapel. He almost sighed. He didn't want to hurt these people, though he supposed his ancestors had not retained their wealth without focusing on their goals.

Miss Georgiana Butterworth was no concern of his, he reminded himself. It didn't matter how pleasantly the light fell on the contours of her cheeks, and it certainly didn't matter how her brown eyes sparkled.

She'd wasted his precious time, leading him to believe she was marrying his brother. If she had done the decent thing and told him, he could have made the same offer to Miss Charlotte Butterworth. Perhaps she would have had some sense; after all, someone must be in possession of it, since the rest of her family seemed devoid of the quality.

Chapter Twelve

"DARLING!" GEORGIANA'S mother's voice bellowed.

Georgiana and Charlotte dashed toward the sound. Evidently, they must have been at the wrong entrance. Relief moved through Georgiana, but when they rounded the corner of the stone building, her mother was frowning.

"The minister isn't here!" Mama exclaimed. "How curious."

"Londoners," their father said. "I knew we should have married her off in Norfolk. I could have married her myself there."

"But this should have worked!" Mama clasped her hands together. "He must be late."

"It seems like there will be a delay," Papa said.

"A delay!" Mama howled. "There must be someone inside!" She banged on a stained-glass window.

"No need to destroy church property." Papa guided her away, and Mother settled inelegantly on the stairs.

Mama's legs tapped nervously, and she beat her fan with vigor, as if more to dispel nervous energy than to keep herself cool.

Georgiana's heart tightened.

Only one person could be responsible for this, and she did not for one moment think that person was the minister.

Lord Hamish.

She should have warned everyone about him. He'd managed to stop this wedding. She wasn't certain how, but she was confident it had occurred.

Fiddle-faddle.

If only she'd warned Charlotte.

She should have informed her parents. Or even the duke himself. The man was amiable enough. Having a brother intent on sabotaging a wedding, even if it entailed risking his own reputation, should have intrigued him. Instead, she'd talked of the weather, even though one only had to pick up any broadsheet to read about the farmers' worry about the lack of sun.

She'd thought by keeping Charlotte away from Lord Hamish, she was ensuring he would not have a chance to convince her not to marry his brother. Instead, he'd concocted another way to stop the wedding.

"It will be fine," Mama said, even as her feet continued to tap a nervous rhythm. "Something for Charlotte to tell her grandchildren."

Her father murmured agreement, but Georgiana paced the outside of the church.

The onlookers definitely seemed suspicious now.

Georgiana felt self-conscious in her finest attire. Most people who dressed in silk and lace didn't do so to stand in front of locked churches at ten o'clock in the morning. Everyone knew the *ton* seldom made an appearance before the afternoon.

A carriage rolled up, and two men stepped outside.

The Duke of Vernon was here and dressed in his finest.

That had to be a good sign. It must mean he intended to marry Charlotte.

"Your Grace! Your Grace!" Georgiana's mother rushed toward the two men. "My dear boy."

"What's all this?" The duke's blue eyes were the symbol of concern, and Georgiana's shoulders relaxed.

It would be absolutely fine.

Perhaps the minister was in fact inside and had had the sudden urge to pray in peace, and they would all laugh about it during the wedding breakfast.

"Where is my bride?" the duke asked cheerfully.

"You mustn't see her!" Mama practically threw herself over Charlotte. "It's bad luck."

"It seems you've already had bad luck," Lord Hamish said. "I'm certain having my brother see the bride will not add to that."

"Oh, you are a gentleman, my lord," her mother breathed, fanning herself. "Isn't he, dear Georgiana?" She turned back to Lord Hamish. "How lucky Charlotte is to be gaining you as a brother. How deeply fortuitous."

Georgiana glanced at him. The man seemed calm.

Was it possible he was *too* calm? *Suspiciously* calm? Why did he seem to know what was going on?

This was, after all, the man who had climbed through her balcony window, hauling more money than she'd seen in her lifetime and attempted to bribe her to call off the wedding. This was the man who'd spent the day before his brother's marriage attempting to malign his own brother.

He'd planned this.

Perhaps he'd locked the minister up in his home. Perhaps he'd bribed him. The man *had* been carrying about a sack with ridiculous amounts of coin.

"The minister isn't here," Mama wailed. "How terribly odd. And some person told us there was a problem with the banns, but I'm certain that must be a mistake."

"Most likely a misunderstanding," the duke said, though Georgiana noted that his eyes drifted to his brother.

He suspects.

"Looks like you'll have to arrange it for another day," Papa said.

"Oh!" Mama clapped her hands together. "That will give me more time to plan. It will be the wedding of the season! Of the decade!"

"I think Princess Charlotte has already claimed that honor," Papa said.

"Such a pity," Mama said.

The duke cast a worried glance at Charlotte. "I don't think we should wait."

"How romantic!" Mama clapped her hands together. "Do something, Mr. Butterworth."

Papa nodded. "I'm going to track down this minister."

"I'll go with you," Lord Hamish said hastily, and the two men disappeared into the Butterworth coach.

Mama sighed contentedly, though Georgiana was not confident the duke's brother would assist the situation.

She swallowed hard and approached the duke. "I must speak with you."

"The dear boy is upset," Mama said. "He doesn't have time."

Georgiana inhaled. "It's important."

"Very well," the duke said. "We can test the doors of the church again."

Georgiana's mother frowned. "But that's all. I don't want you stealing the duke from underneath poor Charlotte's nose."

"That won't happen," Georgiana reassured her.

Mama continued to look dubious.

"Let's check the back doors first," Georgiana said.

The duke nodded, and they rounded the corner.

It was the first time she'd been alone with the duke, and Georgiana was well aware this couldn't precisely count as being alone. There were many people in the square. More of the *ton* had begun to make their morning calls, and some of them gazed curiously at them.

Most likely it was obvious they were dressed for a wedding.

"Your brother wants to stop the wedding," Georgiana blurted, once they were out of her mother's vision.

She tilted her head up at him.

The duke didn't blink.

He certainly didn't flinch.

No surprise seemed to show on his face at all.

"You knew," she said.

"No," the duke said. "But the minister isn't here, and that's the sort of thing to make a man suspicious, given my brother's lack of enthusiasm."

"Then..." She couldn't ask him if the duke still intended to marry Charlotte. Perhaps his brother had convinced him.

The duke gave her a sad smile. "I'm not changing my mind."

Relief swept through her. "Good. I'm sorry to speak ill of your brother. I thought you should know—"

"You were right to tell me."

She nodded, but her face felt tight.

He leaned closer. "What are you not telling me?"

She raised her chin. "I told you everything."

"How exactly do you know my brother was trying to stop the wedding?"

She shifted her feet, wishing her silk slippers were less thin.

"Perhaps you're making it up," the duke said sternly.

"No," Georgiana said hastily. "He thought I was Charlotte and tried to bribe me."

"He didn't have much time to do that," the duke said.

"Er—no."

The duke furrowed his brow. "The driver of his rented post chaise presented himself before my brother arrived. Hamish said he had been wandering the streets. But perhaps he was attempting to stop the wedding?"

"If stopping the wedding involved climbing up to my balcony and breaking into my room," Georgiana said. "And then offering me coin as a bribe not to hold the wedding."

"Damnation."

"To be fair," Georgiana said. "It was a lot of coin."

"That in no manner improves things," the duke said, his voice firm. "Thank you for informing me."

"So once you clear up whatever issue there is with the publication of the banns with a new minister, you can marry again. That should just take a few days." Georgiana beamed. "Or you could even travel to my father's parish in Norfolk, though that will take longer."

They could wait. The important thing is, now the duke knew to be careful, and he wasn't upset with her.

"I don't want to wait a few days," he said.

Georgiana sighed. "I know. It's a shame."

"I'm not interested in marrying here again." His lips twitched. "Or rather, I'm not interested in *attempting* to marry here again."

She blinked. "I don't understand."

"I've always liked the idea of elopement."

"Truly?"

He nodded. "Let me speak to Charlotte."

Excitement thrummed through her. "Can I do anything to help?"

"You can make certain my brother does not follow us."

"I promise." The vow was simple to make, and Georgiana soon strode toward her mother and sister, filled with trepidation and excitement.

People weren't supposed to elope, but the fact the duke was so unconcerned with his brother's machinations against Charlotte and that he still desired to marry her, filled Georgiana's heart with joy.

She'd been foolish to doubt the man's intentions.

"You'll need to tell my mother," Georgiana said. "She'll worry if Charlotte simply disappears."

"Most people don't tell their relatives they plan to elope beforehand."

"Mama's romantic." Georgiana shrugged.

The duke's lips twitched. "I'd gathered that."

The duke spoke first with Charlotte and then with Mama. Georgiana knew the moment when Mama learned, for she let out a shriek, though not of displeasure.

Commoners didn't go to Gretna Green to elope; they waited patiently for the banns to be published.

The duke and Charlotte seemed prepared to depart, but Georgiana stopped them.

"Do you think your brother will believe the wedding is called off?" she asked.

The duke hesitated and shifted his legs. Finally he smiled. "Tell him he can take my carriage. He will believe the wedding has been called off then."

"Are you certain?"

The duke shrugged. "He needs something grander than a rented post chaise to ride back to Scotland anyway. Besides, I have other carriages."

The duke and Charlotte left on foot quickly, no doubt hastened by a desire to leave before Papa and the duke's brother arrived back and before Mama could contemplate the ramifications of her youngest daughter eloping with the duke.

All would be fine if they did marry...but what if they didn't?

Georgiana pushed that thought aside. They would marry...as long as Lord Hamish did not discover where they were going and stop the wedding. He had succeeded in hindering one wedding, who knew what he could do if given the chance?

They left and Mama and Georgiana watched the Butterworth coach arrive, swerving over the tilestones with rather more force than the gentle glide with which it had arrived at the church. The coach stopped, and the door swung open. Papa stepped out, his cravat disheveled despite Mama's earlier efforts.

"I couldn't find the minister, but it seems like the wedding cannot happen today," Papa said, his voice carrying with the ease of a man accustomed to speaking to a large congregation.

The other people in the square leaned forward, evidently finding the lack of a wedding shocking.

"Remember, don't tell them about the elopement. Not yet," Georgiana whispered.

Mama nodded.

They didn't just have to worry about Lord Hamish. Papa would try to stop the elopement if he knew his youngest daughter was going to take a multi-day journey with a man to whom she was not married.

Georgiana's stomach felt somewhat queasy. Perhaps she'd made a mistake. Perhaps she never should have encouraged the elopement.

"There will be no wedding," Mama said.

Lord Hamish looked like he was attempting to keep from beaming.

"I don't understand," Papa said.

"The duke told us," Mama said, looking at Georgiana.

Georgiana nodded. "He said he changed his mind."

"Where is Charlotte?" Papa asked.

There was a moment of silence, and then Georgiana said, "Crying."

"Poor girl," Papa said. "I still don't understand."

"Where is my brother?" Lord Hamish asked.

"I'm afraid the man did not want to spend time with us. He mentioned wanting to walk."

"But the dear man said you might take the coach all the way to Scotland," Mama added.

"He said something about the coach being best at the family estate," Georgiana added. "He didn't want you to have to rent a post chaise again."

The duke's brother beamed, then forced a more somber expression on his face.

Papa glowered at Lord Hamish. "Were you behind this?"

Lord Hamish averted his gaze, though his back was too straight and his chest too upright to appropriately mimic shame. "I should leave you alone."

Georgiana watched the duke's brother walk away.

Neighing sounded behind her. Rows of horses waited patiently for their owners to return, their carriages still attached to them. Some of them had golden family crests, and others had bright carriage wheels that must prove challenging for the groomsmen to clean. Georgiana suspected that even the wheels of the most aristocratic carriages must still happen upon debris and mud. Even the highest of the *ton* wouldn't be able to change the weather.

Something caught her eye. A tartan blanket fluttered in the wind, and her lips twitched.

London might be filled with recently arrived immigrants from the wars on the continents, but it was entirely less in possession of Scots. The English had banned the display of tartan in the last century, and there would be few Scots who might so brazenly display it now.

It was the sort of thing the younger brother of a duke might leave.

That was obviously the duke's coach, and now it was Lord Hamish's.

A horrible thought occurred to Georgiana.

If he went to the duke's home and didn't find him, he would suspect the duke was eloping with Charlotte.

Georgiana's heart shuddered.

It was up to her to stop Lord Hamish from stopping the wedding. She'd promised the duke.

A plan occurred to her.

A *brilliant* plan.

She could sneak into the coach. Once sufficient time had passed that he wouldn't be able to catch up with Charlotte and the duke were he to return, she would announce her presence, and the duke's brother would be honor-bound to take her back to her parents.

He wouldn't want any rumors to happen about them.

Most likely he would find some woman on the street to impersonate a chaperone on the way back to London, just to remain on the correct side of propriety.

She turned to her mother. "I'm going to join Charlotte."

"Excuse me?" Mama's eyes were wide, but thankfully she refrained from revealing Charlotte's location.

Georgiana nodded. "She needs me."

"Good idea, my dear," Papa said, and Georgiana hurried away.

She approached the coach, careful to avoid being seen by the duke's brother.

She tried the door, and thankfully it opened.

Georgiana slid the blanket over herself and slipped underneath the seat, pressing against the cold carriage wall. The air was still chilly, as if uncertain whether it desired to bluster the north wind about, tossing and turning everything in its path with the glee of a boy still in a skeleton suit.

Finally footsteps sounded on the cobblestones outside. The footsteps turned, and someone pulled himself up to the top of the coach.

Lord Hamish.

The coach soon began to roll over the cobblestones, accompanied by the trot of two pairs of horses.

Fear prickled through Georgiana, but it didn't matter. This was for her sister and the duke.

She could call out for the coach to stop, but she didn't want a passing servant or acquaintance to see her. The carriage hardly looked discreet.

When the coach picked up speed, she crawled out from underneath the seat and sat atop it. She draped a tartan blanket over her head, disguising her auburn hair should anyone she knew pass by.

The carriage lurched and jolted, rounding corners and stopping abruptly. Lord Hamish was evidently not a proponent of caution. Georgiana resisted the temptation to leap from the carriage and find a hack in which to return. Her family was depending on her, whether they were aware or not.

Finally, the coach's speed steadied and the world quieted. They must have left the chaos and clamor of the capital, and she peeked through the window. The distances between the buildings had widened, and they must be on the Great North Road.

She reminded herself this was a good thing and pushed away the fear that rose up through her. Once Hamish stopped the coach to change horses, she would make her presence known. The man would be compelled to return her and would lose his chance of preventing the wedding from occurring again.

Chapter Thirteen

AS THE STREETS OF LONDON flew by, Hamish waited for his chest to brim with pride.

The sensation failed to arrive.

No matter.

It would. If he felt a slight ache inside, well that didn't mean it had to do with guilt. Most likely it only meant he was sorry there hadn't been a wedding breakfast.

He held the reins loosely, pulling on the leather only when the horses needed to change streets.

The sun still shone brightly, and Hamish basked in the bright light. He would almost miss London. The city had more parks than he'd imagined. The homes in Mayfair tended to surround verdant squares, and Hyde Park, with its large leafy trees and languid, artificial lake was nearby.

He passed narrow townhouses, imbued with heavy facades, as if an abundance of Doric columns might make up for their diminutive size.

In a week he would be back in the Highlands, and he would be able to work further on his designs.

It might be ten o'clock, when any farmhand had been up for hours, but it was still early for the *ton*. They would be inside, possibly trying to avoid spilling chocolate on their white gowns or cravats, the most athletic accomplishment of their day.

For their servants' sakes, Hamish hoped Mayfair would be filled with triumph this morning.

He left the sumptuous surroundings of Mayfair, and the road widened. The fact did not mean the horses could quicken their speed: servants and tradesmen, urchins and beggars lined the streets. Thin men of a certain age who'd most likely fought valiantly at Waterloo a year ago now shivered or slept along the road. Vehicles thronged the streets. Private crests that marked the finest private carriages gleamed amidst common hacks and wagons.

Hamish settled back on his perch, reliving his success.

He shifted his legs.

Perhaps it was best not to do that.

That strange gnawing feeling occurred in his chest again.

Guilt.

Hamish forced his mind to think of other things, such as the stability he'd just bestowed upon Callum's unborn children. They would have Montgomery Castle to play in, and their wealth would be secure. Generations of future Montgomerys would shudder at how near they'd come to disaster.

Perhaps Callum was upset now, but at some point he'd be grateful and he'd admit Hamish's superiorly developed foresight.

The spaces between buildings eventually grew larger, and swathes of fields lay before Hamish.

He had exited London, the site from which so many British kings and queens had plotted the destruction of their northern neighbor, ordering deadly invasions with the casualness which they normally may have directed toward pesky wasps.

Soon, he would be in Scotland. All that lay between him were some nights in posting inns. He wouldn't have to dance waltzes with inconveniently alluring women and he certainly wouldn't have to make conversation. He could even spend the evenings working on his architectural designs.

He waited again for the relief to arrive.

Instead, the day stretched on, and the buildings turned honey-colored, as if to mimic the appearance of sunshine and brightness. The trot of the horses grew less assured, and when Hamish spotted a posting inn, he guided the team to it. He parked the carriage in the courtyard and arranged for a silvery haired groom to change the horses. Perhaps he would be able to hire a driver here, though the distraction of driving was not altogether unpleasant.

Hamish sauntered inside the pub. Large timbers criss-crossed along the wall, though their substantial size had evidently not kept the walls from sloping inward. His finger itched. He was eager to return to his drafting table and all normalcy.

Something hearty was definitely called for. Unfortunately, the menu was devoid of so much as a bridie, that great Scottish pasty. He'd have to satisfy himself with a cold collation. Hopefully, it included some poultry. Nothing surpassed meat in taste. He thought longingly of the tongue and ham and eggs that would have been served at the wedding breakfast. *No matter.* He was happy to have sacrificed that cursory pleasure.

Now was not the time to tarry. He'd be a fool to attempt to travel in the dark, and he didn't want to waste time in England. He may have stopped the wedding, he may have saved future generations from anguish, but he still needed to return. He needed to finish his commission, and the estate required his attention. No steward could care about the estate as much as he did.

The sun continued to shine when he left the posting inn, and he grinned as he approached the carriage. Fresh horses were hooked onto it, and they stood, swinging their tails, stomping their hooves and snorting.

He nodded at the groom. "Thank you."

The groom had a strange expression on his face.

It seemed almost...disapproving.

Hamish sighed. Most likely his Scottish accent had put the man off. He would have thought the groom would have noticed his accent before, but now was not the time to ponder the limits of English intelligence.

Hamish had wanted to inquire about a driver, but he decided against it, lest the man declare no driver would desire to visit Scotland or some other such nonsense. Perhaps he'd inquire at the next posting inn.

He neared the carriage. Some woman was wearing a bright yellow dress on the other side. He hardly thought this posting inn was worthy of fine attire. Most women were clothed in sensible traveling gowns, the drab colors suited for the inevitable mud and dust that would upon them.

In fact, the dress looked rather like something someone might wear for a wedding. Miss Butterworth had worn something quite similar. *Remarkably* similar. The same yellow with the same net overlay. Even the woman's ivory slippers appeared the same, though Hamish supposed that if one had the poor sense to attempt travel in a flimsy fabric certain to be pierced easily, one most likely also had the poor sense to attempt travel in ivory slippers. The glossy sheen looked very like silk, and he had a moment of sympathy for the hardworking silkworms who'd toiled over the thread and the merchants who'd arranged transport for it from some far-flung Chinese port only for the shoes to be slathered in Cambridgeshire mud.

Perhaps the elder Miss Butterworth was regretting not accepting the proffered coin on behalf of her sister when she'd the chance. *Oh, well.* He'd had a duty to the Montgomery name. One day he hoped she would understand. Besides, her opinion didn't matter. He'd never see her again.

Hamish hardened his jaw and approached the coach. He glanced again at the dress, whose owner had decided to move.

The dress truly resembled Miss Butterworth's. Obviously, it must be a delusion. He'd spent so much time with the Butterworth family, his mind evidently was accustomed to thinking about them. Most likely Miss Butterworth had actually worn a blue dress with no netting at all, and his mind shouldn't be musing over her in the slightest.

All the same, he swung his gaze about the carriage park of the posting inn. None of the scruffy carts resembled something the Butterworth family might travel in, and he ascended to the coach's perch.

"Lord Hamish," a female voice said.

The voice sounded familiar, and Hamish's heart stopped.

He thought again of the dress...of the shoes.

"Lord Hamish!" the voice said again.

Hamish turned.

Miss Butterworth was before him.

At least, this woman had the same auburn hair, the same wide-set eyes, and the same yellow, wildly inappropriate dress.

"What are you doing here?" His voice sounded hoarse, and he coughed.

"I'm afraid I fell asleep in the coach," she said. "You'll have to bring me back to London. I am sorry. How silly of me."

The one thing he knew about Miss Butterworth was that she was not silly. He rolled his gaze over her, but she managed to maintain an innocent expression. Still... Her words sounded almost...rehearsed.

Why on earth would Miss Butterworth have claimed to fall asleep inside his coach if she hadn't?

"You're too intelligent to do that."

She paused for a moment, but then she gave a slight giggle. "How kind of you to say that."

He narrowed his eyes. "Why did you enter my coach?"

"Well, I was ever so exhausted." Her lashes fluttered at a distinctly faster pace than normal.

Outrageous.

She was attempting to flirt with him, even though she didn't like him. She was behaving most suspiciously.

He glanced in the direction of the posting inn to see his reflection.

No.

He had not become more attractive since this morning and he would have had to get substantially more attractive for her to be fluttering her lashes at such a rate. Since the lassie had spent the majority of their conversations berating him, she would have had to have undergone a considerable personality shift as well.

"What are you not sharing with me?" He glowered, and her eyes widened in a predictable manner.

From the distance he spotted the groom. The man was frowning and approaching.

Most likely the groom thought they were having a marital dispute. Well, he didn't have time to defend himself. They needed to leave.

Hamish scowled. "Get up."

Miss Butterworth blinked. "Excuse me?"

He grabbed her hand and pulled her onto the seat, conscious of soft curves and shifting fabric.

"W-What are you doing?" Miss Butterworth stammered.

The lassie retained such a startled expression, that he grinned. "My muscular frame is not just for show."

Her face pinkened in a delightful manner, and he focused on the reins, and not the fact that Miss Butterworth and he were wedged tightly together.

Hamish urged the horses to trot, and they left the posting inn.

"We're going in the wrong direction," she exclaimed. "We should head back to London."

He smirked. "Is that so?"

"Yes," she squeaked.

He pondered what would have compelled her to have sneaked into his carriage.

"Are you attempting to compromise me, lassie?" he asked.

"Me? Compromise you?" She scooted away. "That would be nonsense. Quite impossible. How could you think such a thing?"

Hmph.

"I would make an excellent husband," he grumbled.

Her eyes widened, and warmth stung his cheeks. "I only meant you needn't be outraged."

"Oh."

And then another thought occurred to him. If Miss Butterworth did not intend to spend time *with* him, perhaps she intended him to stay *away* from something. Miss Butterworth seemed eager to return to London. Had she snuck onto his coach purely so he would have to return her, knowing he would be unlikely to let her risk harm by attempting to travel back alone?

For some reason, she didn't want him to go to Scotland. He scrunched his eyebrows together.

Gretna Green.

The thought leaped through his mind. The small village had profited from the Hardwick Act of 1754 and had gained notoriety throughout the British Isles as a haven for inappropriate weddings. Callum must be planning to take his bride there.

It all made sense. His brother hadn't given up on Miss Charlotte Butterworth after all.

Hamish's chest ached. Not only had his brother not respected his opinion—he'd lied.

"My brother still intends to marry your sister," Hamish said.

Miss Butterworth was silent.

She would have let him know if he was wrong. His lips almost quirked. They would have quirked if he'd been slightly less angry.

"They intend to elope in Scotland, where they won't need a marriage license," he said.

She remained silent.

God in heaven.

Hamish tightened his grip on the reins, and his knuckles whitened. "My brother lied to me."

"I'm sorry," Miss Butterworth said finally. "I imagine it must be hard for you."

"It is," Hamish said. "I'm his brother."

"He was worried you would try to stop the next wedding, so he—"

"Lied to me," Hamish finished.

His voice wobbled uncharacteristically. Callum was his twin. He wasn't supposed to lie to him. They didn't have parents. Even their guardians were now gone. Whom did they have except each other?

Callum has Miss Charlotte Butterworth.

The thought had been absurd. Callum and the other Miss Butterworth hadn't acted as if they were a love match, but had Hamish been blind to everything except his preconceptions?

For the first time he was unsure.

Either way he had to speak to his brother. He wasn't going to allow Callum to marry on a whim or an act of rebellion. Hamish had always been the stable one, and Callum had always been incorrigible. Callum had always been thankful when Hamish had stepped in and saved things. Why wouldn't he be now?

Miss Butterworth shifted on the seat, and the wood creaked below them.

"Damnation." Hamish scowled.

She gasped.

"You can't tell me such dreadful things and expect me not to be upset," Hamish said.

"N-Naturally not," Miss Butterfield said, glancing back in the direction of the capital.

He urged the horses to go faster. He needed to get to Scotland.

At once.

Chapter Fourteen

GEORGIANA WAS COMING to the dreadful realization that her brilliant plan might lack brilliance.

Lord Hamish's gaze remained upon her, like some beast in the woods, assessing whether to attack her now or wait for another occasion. She supposed that warmth had never traditionally been bestowed on bearers of bad news.

She'd thought the duke's brother was galloping in pursuit of the duke and Charlotte, when instead he'd been under the entirely mistaken impression that he'd stopped the wedding. No doubt he'd been heading toward Scotland, spurred on by visions of bannocks, bridies, and black pudding.

And now...

Well, she wasn't certain what would happen now, but he was not turning the carriage around.

She cleared her throat. "Naturally you'll need to return me to my parents."

"Is that so?"

"Yes. A gentleman should not be alone with a lady."

"I'm Scottish, lassie. I didn't think I was considered a gentleman."

"Of course you are," she said.

He glanced at her, but his smile had vanished. "I'm not returning you."

"You're jesting."

"I'm not," he said, his voice serious.

Her heartbeat seemed to have caught up with the implications of his words, for it had started to beat much more rapidly.

She glanced down at the ground, wondering just how quickly the carriage was going. Would it hurt if she leaped from it?

If only she weren't wearing such a frilly dress. The puffed sleeves might be fashionable in London, but she had the impression the style had not yet conquered the counties, and people might view the netting as a sign of a person they could take advantage of, despite its expedient manner in adding volume. The carefully stitched flowers on the hem would not prevent any ruffians from harming her and would only serve to make her stand out to every person with nefarious intentions.

She should be in her traveling gown. She'd never longed for a dreary brown dress more.

HAMISH SCOWLED.

The lass had sneaked into the coach out of some misguided sense of duty. It was dashed inconvenient. Had she really thought that by flinging herself into his carriage he would return her to her parents? She'd acted too quickly, too impetuously. He wouldn't change his plan for her, no matter how innocent she might appear with her widely spaced eyes, and no matter how fetching her habit of wobbling her lower lip when distressed might be.

"I'll scream," she said. "You can't take me with you against my will."

Her voice was firm, and he almost wanted to smile, but he noticed the slight wobble of her lips.

She was scared.

God in heaven. He'd scared her.

"I won't hurt you," he promised. "I won't ever hurt you. That's not the sort of man I am. You have to believe that, but I can't take you back to London. Not when it entails abandoning my brother to a terrible fate."

She straightened and narrowed her eyes.

"Not that your sister is unpleasant," he hastened to add. "But she's not his betrothed, and I see no reason to hamper relations with the McIntyre family. I'm not going to let him destroy centuries of good relations with our nearest neighbor." *Or sadden the ghosts of our finest guardians.* "Lady Isla has done nothing wrong. She doesn't deserve to have her reputation smeared."

"This has nothing to do with this Lady Isla."

He gave her a long hard stare. "Even you don't believe that."

She swallowed hard.

"You've heard about Lady Cordelia?" he asked more casually.

"Daughter of the Duke of Belmonte? Loveliest debutante of this century?" Her voice had a bitter edge to it which he despised.

"That must be an exaggeration," he said.

"Why?"

Because it didn't include you.

He kept the compliment on his tongue and averted his gaze. "Lady Cordelia's reputation was maligned after she was betrothed to two men. Neither time led to a marriage."

"Perhaps Lady Isla can be clever enough to marry the next man to whom she is promised," Miss Butterworth said. "Besides, why would I wish my sister's reputation to be maligned?"

Hamish gritted his teeth together. She was as loyal to her sister as he was to his brother. It was damned inconvenient. "You have to let me speak with him again."

"You had your chance," Miss Butterworth said airily.

"Then I want another one. You must understand. I won't give up until there's no more hope."

Tears welled in her eyes.

He sighed. "Look. Once we meet with your sister, she can vouch for you and say you were traveling with her. She'll protect your reputation. If you scream and people learn you were traveling alone with me... will that help you?"

She was silent, then slowly shook her head. "No. But that's not how this was supposed to work."

"Aye." He shrugged. "But that's how it does work, lassie. It would be foolish of me to *not* try to take advantage of it."

"You're a horrible man."

He flinched, but then shot her a lazy smile. "I can drop you at the next posting inn and give you the fare for the mail coach. What will going back alone gain you?"

She was silent, but he answered for her anyway. "Nothing."

"You're right," she admitted.

"Aye, so I am."

If she continued on with him, her sister could salvage her reputation. People would believe Miss Butterworth had helped her sister elope, and the word of a duchess meant something. Her reputation would be destroyed if she were spotted arriving in London by herself or if someone decided to take advantage of her.

Hamish urged the horses forward. The flat landscapes provided expansive views of the Great North Road and the long column of wagons and gigs that filled it.

Wind swept over them, the force stronger given their high, unprotected perch. Miss Butterworth placed her hands over her dress, protecting the frivolous material from lifting in unladylike manners. "We'll need to get two rooms in posting inns."

"Naturally," he grumbled.

"And you're going to behave."

"Like a choir boy. Though you shouldn't be making the rules. This is my coach, after all."

"What do you want?" she asked, her voice tentative.

There was something appealing about how her face changed color with her emotions. She was beautiful all the time, but he loved how her skin reddened when she was angry and paled when she was distressed.

He shook his head. He shouldn't be contemplating her. "I don't need to make conversation with you for the next four hundred miles."

She nodded miserably.

God in heaven.

He'd been too harsh, but how was he supposed to travel with her all the way to Scotland?

Chapter Fifteen

GEORGIANA CLOSED HER eyes, willing herself to pretend that she was still in Norfolk. But the ever-winding road could not be confused with Norfolk's flat terrain, and the sounds of other coaches and horses trotting could not be confused with the gentle hum of her father's vicarage.

The horror of what she'd done moved through her, but she raised her chin. This could still work. He would bring her to Charlotte, since he desired to see the duke.

Everything *could* be fine.

It has to be.

The coach slowed and then veered to the side. Lord Hamish could be heard soothing the horses.

What had caused him to stop?

Georgiana's heartbeat quickened, and she was conscious that she was not supposed to be here. Was this when the man decided to ravish her? Tension swept through her body, and she reminded herself that ravishment would be by no means desirable.

She could hear his footsteps nearby, and she stiffened. He opened the door. The sun hung low on the horizon, as if to better direct its rays into her eyes.

She forced a smile on her face, as if she were having a pleasant time inside the coach and were not the least bit afraid. She wondered if men could smell fear. Couldn't animals? Would he take advantage of her?

"Out," Lord Hamish said, his voice rough.

"Pardon me?"

He sighed. "You can't stay in that coach the whole day."

"But I intend to!"

"The weather is nice," he said. "You shouldn't be inside. At least, not on my account. No one's going to recognize you so far from London."

Georgiana frowned and exited the coach. She followed him up to the perch.

"A break from the rain is a cause to celebrate," he said.

Georgiana was silent. He didn't need to know she felt any relief at leaving the coach's drab, dark interior.

The wagons and gigs that had filled the road had thinned, as if few people could discern a reason to be so far from the capital. Villages were visible in the distance, their stone homes from past centuries clustered around plump Norman churches. The poor weather had not been conducive to the creation of an appropriate floral environment. Still, it was June, and even if some of the orchards remained bare, damaged from the harsh climate, and even if there were rather fewer flowers than the year before, there were still flowers, and it was still lovely.

He grinned. "I thought a garden enthusiast would favor being outside."

The man needn't look so proud, and she willed her facial features to display rather less enthusiasm. Despite the pleasant surroundings, the fact remained that he was ushering her away from everything she knew.

"I still consider myself to be captured," Georgiana said.

"You have made my job too easy for that to be correct," he said.

"Why don't you want your brother to be happy?"

He blinked. "But I do want that. Everything I am doing is for his good."

"He can be happy marrying the woman he loves."

"Didn't you find it odd that they barely spoke to each other?"

The man might actually have a point, but Charlotte was hardly the bubbly type, and the duke was evidently the strong and silent type. Besides, Mother was quite capable of chattering enough for both of them.

Georgiana raised her chin. "Their passion needs no words."

"You know about passion, lassie?"

She despised that his voice managed to be so mocking, and she despised more that the words seemed to have some strange impression on her body.

It was the word passion, she decided. It was a word utterly lacking in propriety, and if she shivered, it was just in revulsion.

"I don't matter," she said. "They do. Please do not commit them to a lifetime of misery."

He blinked, and for a moment something like respect flickered in his eyes. "It's not just about the money."

"Of course not. How could you think that?"

"But your family—" His cheeks reddened. "They don't—" He looked down again, obviously embarrassed, and she gave an exasperated sigh.

He could be embarrassed. That was fine. She wasn't going to lessen his unease.

"Don't you think they might be forcing my brother to marry your sister because of my brother's more established—er—finances?"

"Nonsense."

"It's the truth."

"You're making assumptions."

Bewilderment leaped over his face, and she sighed. "First of all... I doubt my parents could force your brother to do anything. Papa was never even in the local militia, and he's hardly a source for bribes."

"Well—"

"Moreover—" She tossed her hair, and his eyes widened, sending a definitely inappropriate thrill through her. "If my parents had such an interest in money, wouldn't they have achieved it by now?"

"I don't think it's that easy—"

"Well, my mother could have married someone else. A vicar's studious second son is hardly mistaken for being a source of riches. And Father? Well, Father isn't forced to devote himself to fading leather tomes. He enjoys it. In fact," and she allowed herself a smile, "He's rather an expert."

"I see."

"They're really quite wonderful," she said. "But you understand. Your family—"

His skin paled, and she looked down hastily. Too late she remembered that his family was dead, had died so long ago that he might not even remember them.

"You mean I wouldn't know anything about families?"

She flinched at the slight sarcasm in his voice. "I'm sorry."

The man's facial muscles seemed too tight, but he gave a curt nod. "There's a posting inn here. I think we better get out and eat."

"Good idea," she said brightly, as if smiling might keep guilt from churning in her stomach.

The posting inn was a small structure that looked as if it had been pieced together rapidly in the hopes of serving passengers.

She missed the friendly half-timbered coaching inns that sat majestically in some parts of the countryside as if they'd been around for centuries, and would remain for centuries more, unruffled by even the most eccentric guest. Those coaching inns had thatched roofs and window boxes.

This place didn't even have windows; evidently the owner had seen no need to get taxed for something as intangible as natural light.

Lord Hamish guided the horses into the courtyard. When he stepped down, she didn't take his proffered hand. The ground might seem awfully far away, and a groom might usually assist her, but he needn't think her so helpless that she couldn't disembark on her own.

The speed at which she descended the coach was *perhaps* quicker than normal. Her feet crunched against the gravel, and she glanced warily at the wagons, carts and vans parked outside. More donkeys than horses were present, and some of the male guests had wandered outside, still clasping their tin tankards.

"Oooh!" Some of the men shouted and pointed in their direction.

Lord Hamish's face paled, and he halted. "Follow me." He dashed back to the coach, jerked open the door and removed the blanket. "Wrap this around your shoulders. You'll look just like any other woman."

He spread the fabric over her. He smoothed his fingers along it, and warmth that could not be entirely attributed to the woolen material spread through her. Georgiana held the blanket's corners as if it were a cloak, simply missing its buttons.

"You resembled a cake confection," he explained. "Something some French patisserie concocted from sugar."

Georgiana flushed. "And the men don't enjoy cake confections?"

He looked puzzled for a moment, and then he shook his head. "I'm afraid these men might be overly fond of them."

Chapter Sixteen

THEY WERE TROUBLE.

Hamish recognized their type at once.

They were loud and drunk and there were too many of them. One of them might prefer to concentrate on his tankard, two of them might grumble to each other or set out to seduce one of the barmaids, but three of them were a force to encourage one another on toward disaster.

Unfortunately, there were more than three.

He hurried Miss Butterworth along. He'd done his best to make Miss Butterworth look less radiant, less beautiful, less glamorous, even though he'd felt terrible covering up her dress. She shouldn't change anything about herself for these wretched men, but when they neared them, the men started to call out names of such vulgarity that Miss Butterworth's face paled.

The only comfort was that the words possessed such vileness, he doubted Miss Butterworth knew them.

Hamish wanted to return to the coach, but the horses needed to be changed, and he hoped that waiting inside, in a place overseen by barmaids who might desire some modicum of order, might be more pleasant.

They soon entered the inn. Despite the fact that the structure was new, it had taken a traditional view on measurements, and Hamish had to duck as he entered. The white walls lacked charm. People clustered at tables and ate.

Hamish turned to Miss Butterworth. "Any preference in food?"

She shook her head.

"Two hot meals," he declared to the barmaid, who directed them to a rickety table near the bar.

Miss Butterworth and he sat down.

The people in the pub were only slightly more proper than people lingering in the courtyard. Evidently the food was a suitable distraction to them.

Still, Hamish was uneasy. Miss Butterworth didn't belong in a location like this. Perhaps she'd not come from money, but she was a vicar's daughter.

"If anyone asks, you're my sister," Hamish whispered.

"Then I was far better at learning the accent." Miss Butterworth's dark eyes glimmered, and he mused again over the discovery that brown eyes were decidedly not dull.

His cheeks warmed, but he smiled all the same. "Perhaps we had different fathers."

"How scandalous." Miss Butterworth widened her eyes. "Did my mother decide to run off with a swarthy pirate?"

"Red-headed pirate, it would seem, though I don't think it would be good to spread about the idea that your mother had low standards in men."

"Pirates can be most under appreciated."

"Yes," he said. "All that pillaging they do. Quite unfairly seen."

"At least they're skilled at something," Miss Butterworth said. "Sailing, swordsmanship, shooting..."

He stretched back, assessing her. "That's an unusual sentiment for a young lady in London to have."

"I'm not from London," she said, "though perhaps you would benefit from spending more time there. We're not as silly as everyone makes us out to be."

"Is that so?" He raised an eyebrow.

"Yes. We have this dreadful reputation for frivolity, but we're not permitted to do anything else. Why wouldn't we become accomplished at the few things that are permitted us?"

"Like garden design?"

"I'm lucky. Papa has always been most tolerant of my desires to tear up and reshape the world around me. He holds neither fresh air nor exercise with suspicion, even when it pertains to women."

"And what intrigues you about garden design?"

"Everything. The task of enhancing a space, to make it the loveliest it can be, is delightful." Her eyes glazed, as if envisioning her work, but then she smiled. "But it's possible Father simply favored a quieter house and was happy for me to go outside. Quiet is more conducive to sermon writing. Or simply reading."

Hamish chuckled. He could imagine that. He'd seen the number and variety of books in the London townhouse. No doubt their actual home contained much more.

"And your sister?"

"She's less enthusiastic about shoveling mud about, though that could be a sign of her greater intellect. She prefers mathematical formulae."

"Indeed?" Hamish asked, conscious he may have sounded overly surprised. Just because he found mathematical formulae tiresome, at least in comparison with the wonders of geometry, did not mean everyone did.

The barmaid interrupted them with their food. The taste might be dull, but dullness would not extend to the rest of the dinner. Miss Butterworth was like no woman he'd ever met. She was brave, intelligent and not the least bit selfish.

"One of my dearest friends, Louisa Carmichael, is passionate about the ocean and everything in it," Miss Butterworth remarked. "She's created this most delightful contraption to allow one to stay longer underwater."

"How incredible."

"Yes," Miss Butterworth murmured, her tone almost wistful. "Rather more wonderful than a garden."

He shook his head adamantly. "No. Garden design is most intriguing."

She tilted her head. "His Grace did regale us with tales of your architectural triumphs."

"He did?" Hamish had thought his brother hardly knew anything about the commissions he'd undertaken.

"To think you designed a practical castle for someone, with all its intricacies, all its romantic touches..." She smiled. "It must have taken so long."

"It's still being built," he said. "But I started designing buildings years ago. I'd shared my sketches with an acquaintance, and when he inherited..."

"You gave him the designs for your dream home," she finished.

"Aye." The fact seemed less pleasant than it normally did, and he considered his brother's comment about using the Montgomery wealth to build a home of his own. "Perhaps I don't live there, but I can visit. But the main thing is to know that it exists, and it will exist longer than I will. Barring any earthquakes."

"Unlikely."

"The house is of a most sturdy stone." He smirked. "Not like your English chalk."

"We don't actually build homes with it."

"You just pontificate about its beauty."

"It is beautiful," she insisted. "There is so much in the natural landscape to enjoy. And if it can be arranged in a manner pleasing to the eye, with specific spaces to wonder at the beauty of nature—"

"I would like to see that."

The air seemed tenser, and she leaned back in her chair. The distance between her shoulders appeared narrower, and her smile vanished. Perhaps she'd remembered they were not actually friends and that he was the man who was preventing her from returning to her family, risking her entire reputation.

His stomach tightened.

He felt much younger around her. Less suave, less sure of himself. Not that he was ever in the habit of feeling suave. Suavity usually demanded leaving one's estate with greater frequency than he did.

Harsh laughter sounded from outside. Those damned men were continuing to drink.

"Perhaps it would be better to say that we're married," he mused, thinking of the men as the commotion grew louder. "Should anyone ask."

She scrutinized him, but finally she nodded. He wondered whether she'd refrained from protesting because she agreed with him, or whether she simply was afraid of him. He certainly hadn't given her any cause to feel safe.

He sighed. Perhaps he should return her to her family after all. Perhaps he'd been wrong.

But it was evening now, and he couldn't very well deliver her in the middle of the night and expect everyone to think she hadn't been compromised.

No.

They might as well continue now. The plan was good. Her sister would vouch for her.

"I'll—er—ask if this place has any rooms," he said.

She frowned, and her eyes flashed with something that was definitely not amusement. "It's still light outside."

"It will get dark."

"The sun isn't even setting."

"But it will happen."

She shook her head. "No. There must be a better option. Can't we drive farther?"

"I'm not sure we'll be able to get to the next coaching inn quickly enough."

"Well, we have to try." Miss Butterworth leaned closer, and an enticing floral scent wafted over him. "I heard what those men said about me."

Right.

He had to think about her safety and not just ponder potential sun patterns.

He stood abruptly, and the chair scraped against the floor. "Then let's go."

She beamed, and he wondered how he could have desired to contradict her. Soon they were outside, and he glanced around to make certain the ruffians were not nearby and guided her quickly to the carriage.

He nodded to the groom. "How far to the next posting inn?"

"It's just in the next village," the groom said. "You can't miss it."

"Splendid," Hamish said. He'd been foolish to worry.

The air was chillier, and he addressed Miss Butterworth. "You should sit inside."

"But—"

"I wouldn't want you to catch cold. That dress is thin, and even with the blanket—"

"I'll sit inside," she said, and even though he was well aware he'd won a debate, he felt as if he'd lost something more.

The horses trotted merrily down the road, evidently happy for some exercise, even if it involved pulling the coach.

He took in the scenery, conscious of missing Miss Butterworth. The sky had continued to resist the temptation to rain, even though it had seemed to do nothing but that all year. The color had turned a more somber gray, resembling the cinder from buildings ceded to cannon fire in the last war.

No matter.

The sky could be gray. It only meant there wouldn't be many stars visible tonight, but Hamish could do without them. They couldn't drive in the night anyway, and he had no expectations of seeing celestial views from whatever room the next posting inn assigned him.

Any moment now he would most likely see signs of the upcoming village, and he waited. Would he see a mill? A hay wain, like in some Constable painting? Or perhaps a manor house perched on one of the few hills in the area?

Hamish scanned the landscape for manor houses.

There were none.

Well, perhaps any manor houses were shielded by tall hedges. Not every manor house could come with a view.

It did seem odd, though, that he wasn't seeing any signs of a village.

He wondered what the source of water would be for the village. Perhaps he would see a river first? Or a lake? Some babbling brook?

The one thing he knew was that he would see some supply of water. Villages had a tendency to consider them vital.

He inhaled the woodsy scent. Some birds chirped.

The village, though, did not come.

Normally this would be fine, but it was growing distinctly dark. The sky's grayness had masked the normal sunset, and the sky hadn't turned tangerine and pink and a display of other colors, all bold and the sort for painters to enjoy. Instead, the sky simply darkened, and he found his eyes straining.

Chapter Seventeen

THE CARRIAGE STOPPED, and Georgiana smiled.

Lord Hamish must have found an inn, and when his footsteps padded from the driver's perch to the door, she pulled the blanket about her shoulders and prepared to leave.

The door opened, and he appeared.

Outside him was only inky darkness, and not the cheerful glow of a coaching inn.

Uncertainty swept through her, and he sat down on the seat opposite. The space diminished in size, and she drew her feet toward her, conscious of long legs, broad shoulders, and a seductive fragrance.

"There's no coaching inn," he said.

"Then keep on going," Georgiana replied.

The answer was simple, but for some reason, the man was not moving.

"It's dark, and the road isn't good. I wouldn't want anything to happen to the horses. I'm sorry."

Oh.

Georgiana's shoulders slumped. Lord Hamish had been riding outside on the perch, but he could hardly be expected to sleep outside. *No.* They would need to share this tiny, compartment which wasn't conducive even to pleasant sitting.

Traveling alone with a man was scandalous, but sleeping in a small, enclosed environment? Far from anyone?

Her heartbeat quickened, but she jutted out her chin and forced her voice to sound confident. "Let's keep on going. The inn is bound to appear soon."

"Very well," he said after a pause. "But we really can't do it for long. This lantern won't last, and it's too dim to be much help for the horses when they're stepping over the road."

"Ten minutes," Georgiana said.

He nodded curtly. Soon the coach jostled to a start, and Georgiana leaned back against her seat. Her heart thrummed with too much force for her to feel relieved. She hoped she'd made the right decision.

Georgiana moved the curtains back and searched the darkness, trying to distinguish if any of the dark shapes in the night might be a building, the sort that would come with warm food and drink and a bed that wouldn't rattle and sway in the night.

Boom.

The horses grunted, and the rhythm of the hooves became more frantic. The coach veered to the side, sending her sliding to the opposite side of the coach. Her shoulder smacked against the hard, polished wood just as he cursed.

She scrambled upright, rubbing her shoulder. The horses continued to neigh, and their hooves continued to pound against the ground, as if scrambling to right themselves.

Georgiana's heart lurched in her chest.

The sound had been too large, but more worrisome was the fact that the coach was no longer moving.

It was supposed to be moving.

They wouldn't be able to reach the next posting inn if the carriage couldn't move, and right now proceeding even a few measly yards seemed an insurmountable feat.

Georgiana pushed open the door and rushed outside. For the first time the ground did not seem far away, but her reaction was not joy.

"Are we stuck?" Georgiana asked in a small voice.

"Aye." He hopped onto the ground and grabbed the lantern. "I'll examine it."

The golden glow of the lantern moved with him, leaving her in darkness. A blustery wind fluttered her clothes, and she wrapped her arms around her. She'd heard the wind pattering against the carriage, but she'd hoped part of its force could be attributed to their speed.

She couldn't retain the same hope now.

It was cold and dark.

And they were alone.

"How is it going?" she asked.

"Not good. A wheel is broken."

"And I don't suppose there's a spare?" Her voice squeaked. Guilt and hopelessness weighed against her chest, rendering any speaking a challenge.

"No."

Right.

Georgiana supposed wheels were rather too large and too cumbersome to make riding with spares a common practice, but disappointment still moved through her.

"Let me look." She stumbled over the uneven ground.

"Suit yourself."

Her feet wobbled over the path, abundantly scattered with stones and tree roots, and she made her way to the lantern.

"See?" He moved the lantern lower and handed it to her.

It wasn't a hallucination.

The wheel was broken.

"We'll find someone to fix it in the morning when it's light," he said.

"And where do you expect us to sleep?"

Georgiana abhorred the wobble in her voice and the fact that it had ascended an octave.

"It will have to be in the coach," he said. "I'm sorry. I wish we could be at an inn too, but I don't see another option."

She crossed her arms. "You're supposed to take me back. That was the plan."

"Well, it didn't work."

She was alone with a man.

At night.

Secluded from everybody and everything.

This wasn't what was supposed to happen, despite the fact that he seemed to be under the impression that she was strong,

"We'll be on our way to Gretna Green in no time. You'll see. Besides, I've already seen you in your night rail," he murmured.

"You mustn't remind me of that." Georgiana's voice was miserable. "That was through no fault of mine."

There had been women at her finishing school who interested themselves in men, who'd been sent to the school after sneaking kisses with footmen and grooms.

But that had never been Georgiana. She'd tried to behave. In fact—it had been easy to behave. Temptation had never presented itself to her. But now a multitude of things could happen. She couldn't simply curl up beside him and sleep.

Georgiana jerked her head, colliding with his arm. She tried to shake off the man's always seductive fragrance. "There's always a way."

"And what do you suggest?" He crossed his arms, and his voice was icy.

"I'll find the posting inn." She turned, but he gripped her arm, sending warmth jolting through her. She struggled from his grasp.

This was the countryside. She should be able to roam about over dewy meadows and wildflowers.

"It's dark," he said, his voice stern.

"I've noticed." She stepped back, and a twig snapped beneath her.

"Naturally. But you can't abandon the coach." He stepped toward her, forcing her to tilt her head up.

"I'll come back," she said hastily. "And I can't spend the night here, alone."

"With me," he finished for her, but the sternness of his voice had disappeared.

Was he remembering their first meeting? Was he remembering the feel of her bosom pressed against his chest, and of how his arms had wrapped around her waist? Was he remembering the feel of her lips against his? Of her taste?

Doubtless, he was in the habit of kissing women like that. He strode with the confidence of a man who never questioned his appeal, who was certain his presence alone would suffice in bringing people joy.

She refused to succumb to his appeal. She needed her own room or even one that she might share with the servant girls of the various travelers. That would suffice. She wasn't asking for much; she just wanted to be away from him.

This was the man who'd worked to destroy her sister's marriage before it even had a chance to happen. This was the man who'd sneaked into her room in the night, not caring about any rules of propriety or her fear. If her parents had discovered him there, she might have been forced to marry him.

Georgiana reminded herself that there could be no worse fate.

No, perhaps they would need to travel with each other, but that would be in daylight.

She'd be a fool to trust him.

"I'll be back in the morning." She marched away from him, widening her strides.

"Georgiana!"

It was the first time he'd called her by her first name, and she wondered if he'd elected to do so now out of expediency or if he'd been referring to her by that name in his mind all along.

No matter.

It was not the sort of thing to mull over.

"You mustn't go!" Lord Hamish called again, but his voice had already grown fainter, and Georgiana smiled. At least she was making good speed. She rushed down the road, floundering over the occasional root. She had a moment of longing for London's cobbled streets. Dirt roads were occasionally less bumpy, but after a rain shower deep grooves could furrow into the dirt.

This lane had evidently seen many rain showers.

If only there'd been a second lantern.

Or perhaps she should have taken the only lantern. Lord Hamish had been intent, after all, on staying by the coach. She quirked a smile, wondering just what compilation of Scottish sounding curses he would utter if she'd done that.

She strode forward. Tall hedges lined both sides of the road, and she told herself it was a sign of inhabitants. Or was it a sign of an empty estate which would have no posting inn to serve it? Would highwaymen be lurking in the top of the chestnut trees on the other side of the hedges, eager to jump on passersby in the hopes of expanding their coin?

A shiver, one perhaps not entirely attributable to the frigid temperature, moved through her, but she continued forward.

Chapter Eighteen

SHE WAS GONE.

Hamish had scarcely finished showing her the broken wheel before she fled. Her legs might be of a shorter length than his, but she knew exactly how to use them.

God in heaven.

Hamish should let her remain wherever she'd gone. Let her get eaten by wild wolves or whatever beasts roamed about Cambridgeshire. It would serve her right for sneaking onto his coach. He nodded decisively, but the sense of certainty was not prolonged.

He could hardly let her succumb to danger. When had he become so intimidating that a lassie would rather take her chances with the great wilderness, even if Cambridgeshire at least didn't border an ocean into which she might topple?

Hamish scowled and sprinted after her.

At least the area on either side was flat and any driver would be able to discern the horses' presence relatively quickly, provided the horses had the good sense to whinny or neigh.

Not that this area was likely to have many travelers. Anyone with any sense would already be tucked in at a posting inn. No stagecoaches would be on the road now.

Still, she was out there—alone.

His heart thrashed in his chest, and he dashed in the direction Miss Butterworth had headed in. He pounded over the road. The tall hedges disappeared, replaced by a wooden area. *Dhia-fhèin.* This was hardly an improvement. He raised his lantern, hoping that the glow would reveal her presence.

Nothing.

He shouted her name and crunched over twigs and leaves as he rushed through the forest. If any highwaymen were here, they would know that they were not alone.

They'd driven through fields most of the day, but now, when he needed to find her, they were in a wooded area. The scent of wildflowers should have been pleasant, but it was only a reminder of their isolation. Hamish had never despised the scent of honeysuckle so much.

The lantern's dim light flickered over the surroundings, revealing dark outlines of long, gnarly trees that brushed against his hands when he ran. A scream sounded. He told himself it was just an owl that had caught its prey. It wasn't Miss Butterworth. *It can't be.*

And then he saw her.

She was sitting on a rock. He couldn't see her face, but her back was hunched forward, and her hair had fallen completely loose, perhaps from the exertion of her run.

He stilled. Twigs snapped beneath him, and the sound seemed impossibly loud. Her back tensed, but she did not turn around.

"I won't come with you," Miss Butterworth said, but her voice had rather less determination in it than when she'd last seen him.

"I won't hurt you," he said solemnly. "You're my responsibility now."

She shifted and turned toward the lantern. Her locks fluttered in the wind, contrasting with her unwavering expression. "What does responsibility mean to a man like you?"

Her words were ferocious, and his shoulders slumped. "I'm sorry about the room."

"Is that all you're sorry about?" Her voice trembled.

He took a tentative step forward, but she drew back immediately. He hesitated and raked his hand through his hair. "I'm sorry I broke into your chamber. And I'm sorry I—er—kissed you. I thought you were your sister."

"That doesn't make it better."

"I apologize." He wanted to say that that had been also to test her loyalties, but he wasn't certain, on reflection, whether that had been the case. Something about her had been so vibrant. He'd wanted to kiss her then. He wouldn't have kissed just anyone.

"What about your brother?" she asked.

"What about him?"

Miss Butterworth inhaled, and even in the dark her frustration was obvious. "You tried to take away his betrothed, and then you got him inebriated."

"I'd forgotten that." He smiled, remembering it, and she must have heard some warmth in his voice.

"You shouldn't be proud of that," she said sternly.

"No, you're right. And naturally I wouldn't have really harmed him."

"Hmph."

"Look. Georgiana."

Her eyes widened, and he considered taking the word back, but her name had felt correct on his tongue, no matter if it was similar to the name of the very English monarch.

"I'm not a rake," he said.

She snorted. "Of course you are."

"No," he said solemnly. "I know that's what you think I am, and I know I've given you that impression. I even *tried* to give you that impression. But I'm not one and never have been."

"You burst into my room."

"I lacked expertise in the endeavor." He knew rogues. Lord Rockport, the Marquess of Bancroft, and Sir Miles all were rogues.

He was not one of them.

"Rogues aren't content to stay home and handle estate concerns, and they certainly aren't content to spend the rest of their time designing buildings."

"Oh," she said.

"Just because you are a woman and I am a man, does not mean that I will feel compelled to dismantle your maidenhood."

She flinched, and he sighed. "See, even my vocabulary is not befitting that of a rogue. I'm sure a true rogue would have made some reference to roses and—"

"Rainbows?"

"Aye," he said, feeling his lips move into a grin. "I would never want you to do anything you don't want to do."

"Except kidnap me?"

A new wave of guilt came through him, but rustling sounded, and relief spread through him as she moved near.

"I suppose I'll have to take that chance," she said.

"Look. We are going to spend the night in the coach, and then we are going to travel to Gretna Green together. You will meet your sister, and somehow we'll concoct a story that will maintain your reputation. But I will not harm you. Think of me as your—"

"Soon to be brother-in-law?"

The word brother should not be anywhere near her lips when referring to him. Brother-in-law wasn't even the technical word for what they would be if Callum married her sister, and he was going to do his best so that Callum *wouldn't* marry her sister.

"Think of me as Hamish," he said. "Not a stranger."

"Not a rogue?"

"Well. You may think of me as a tiny bit of a rogue." He smiled. "My masculinity might demand it. But I assure you I only want to protect you."

"Very well, Hamish," she said. Her voice was warmer, as if she were smiling, and he hoped that just maybe everything would be fine.

Only a few more days until Scotland.

THEY TRUDGED BACK TO the coach together. Hamish's lantern illuminated the path, revealing thick gnarly branches that she could have collided into and ditches into which she could have fallen.

An owl hooted, and rabbits scampered away. They knew the forest was dangerous—why hadn't she?

She shivered and pulled the blanket more firmly about her.

She'd been foolish and too impulsive. *Just like always.*

She swallowed hard.

Hamish strode confidently toward the coach, evidently relieved at having found her. His reassurances had been somewhat amusing. He seemed convinced that rogues were only found in the finest parlors and ballrooms in London or Edinburgh, when Georgiana was quite certain that a true rogue was far more likely to be rambling about craggy peaks on the very edge of Britain and doing daring things like disrupting weddings.

They were soon at the carriage, and Hamish opened the door. She slipped inside, and he followed her and settled onto the other side of the carriage.

Cold gusts of wind blew through the interior. The windows and doors which had seemed sturdy on the drive through London and into the countryside, when the coach had moved at fast speeds of five miles an hour, now seemed at risk of blowing off, even though they'd stopped moving. The door rattled against the latch, groaning in a manner not conducive to sleep and in no ways reminiscent of a lullaby. If only they'd stayed at the last posting inn. Georgiana shouldn't have insisted they continue on.

"You were right," Georgiana said mournfully. "I thought there would be something else, another place to stay."

"There probably is something else," Hamish said magnanimously. "Eventually. Maybe even quite soon."

Georgiana nodded.

"Take my coat." He stripped the woolen material away, and even in the dim light she could see his shirt. The ivory color glowed under the moonlight, and his sleeves billowed in ways quite unlike the refined, polished look of his tailcoat.

"I can't wear that," she said.

"And I can't wear it when I know you're cold."

She hesitated for a moment, but then he said, "I'll help you."

He moved across the narrow seat, and in the next moment she was aware of long legs beside hers and that masculine smell of cotton that seemed more distracting than any floral combination a perfumer in Paris could conjure.

He slid his tailcoat over her shoulders and lifted her arms. The action shouldn't have caused her pulse to quicken. His movements didn't differ from when her maid dressed her. The sleeves reached to her wrists, and his hands never touched her skin, and yet the action felt impossibly intimate.

"Now rise," he whispered, and his voice sounded close to her ear.

She shivered.

She did so, and he pulled the tails straight to keep them from wrinkling.

She huddled inside the new material, conscious that the tailcoat's shoulders collapsed over her smaller ones. "I must look ridiculous."

"Nonsense. No one can see you."

THAT PART WASN'T TRUE.

The fact she was ridiculous was nonsense, but she wasn't quite in the dark. Moonlight drifted through the coach windows. It played on Georgiana's cheeks, illuminating the contours of her face in a manner that sent an ache tumbling through his body.

At some point she'd removed the pins from her hair, and her auburn locks, the color now muted, hung over her shoulders, as if to tempt him to touch it.

Vanilla inundated his nostrils. Whoever made coaches should be scolded for their narrow width and short length, for no sensible distance separated them.

He found the blanket she'd used earlier and wrapped it around her shoulders, tucking her hair over it. The silky strands contrasted with the coarse woolen fabric. She shouldn't be here. He should have taken her straight home to her family once he'd seen her.

"Let's get you warm," he whispered.

"I'm f-fine," she said, her voice more high-pitched than normal.

"Your teeth are chattering."

"P-Perhaps." Her voice seemed small.

God in heaven.

He couldn't let her freeze here. He cursed modistes and their habit of making overly thin dresses for women. He tentatively placed his arms around her shoulders. She tensed at his touch, and he almost moved away, but then she relaxed against him.

"Better?" He tucked a strand of her silky hair behind her ear.

"Mm-hmm."

"Good."

They were silent. At some point her teeth stopped chattering, and she no longer shivered. He could have moved his arm away, but it felt right to have it there.

After all, he'd hardly want her to start shivering again. Leaving his arm about her shoulder was truly the sensible thing to do.

"If I hadn't been here, you wouldn't be sleeping in this coach," she said in a small voice.

"Don't worry about me, lassie. It's much better than a tent at Waterloo."

The blanket rustled, and he felt her turn toward him. "I'm sorry you had to go."

"I'm glad I was there."

He'd helped. He'd led troops into battle. His life had been meaningful.

"So you didn't sneak into my coach in the hopes of compromising me?"

"Me compromise you?" Amusement rippled through her voice, and it was easy to imagine the manner in which her lips would be breaking into a wide smile.

God in heaven. If only it were light, and he could see her fully.

Except... If it were light, he would probably be doing something foolish like turning away from her and pretending she didn't affect him at all.

He didn't want to pretend anymore.

Not when they would be in Gretna Green in a few days. Not when he would then disappear.

Chapter Nineteen

GEORGIANA WOKE TO THE feel of something warm against her, and she snuggled closer to the pleasant sensation. Raindrops pattered, and her back felt stiff. She sympathized with her aunts who sometimes complained of back pain. She shifted again, trying to gain a softer position.

Normally this wasn't difficult. Normally she could move her blanket, and for some reason, she couldn't feel a blanket—

She opened her eyes.

She was in a coach.

Not her bed.

And the soft sensation beside her was not some helpful pillow or scrunched up blanket, but a real, live person.

Lord Hamish Montgomery.

She swallowed hard and jerked away from him.

The sensation was evidently enough to cause him to wake up, for in the next moment he was blinking and rubbing his eyes. Then he realized where he was, and she noted the moment when horror flooded his eyes.

Obviously, the man was feeling guilty.

That had to be good.

She rather wished he were still sleeping. The problem with men who were awake was at some point they decided they wanted to speak, and she didn't know how to best respond.

All the same, he was different than she'd imagined.

He'd been almost sweet last night, even though she supposed that hardly rectified the fact he had not returned her to her family.

He stood up, ducking his head once he'd managed to open his eyes and take in the impropriety of their surroundings.

"I—er—should go outside." His voice sounded husky, and he raked a hand through his hair.

She nodded.

He paused. "You should come with me. We'll need to find someone to repair the wheel."

She removed the man's tailcoat and followed him out. The surroundings did not seem as intimidating as they had last night. She noted the wooded area, but she could see it did not stretch out for miles in every direction. Tall hedges surrounded the road, but on the other side were fields that stretched on either side of them. The right-hand side included something that looked very similar to homes.

"I think that's the start of the village," she said.

He grinned. "Aye, lassie. Let's go."

They proceeded toward the dwellings. The road went through the thick woods, but if they cut through the fields, they could reach the buildings soon. A stone wall interrupted some of the hedges, and Hamish led her toward it.

He extended his hand. "It's perhaps not Almack's but—"

"It's just what I desired," she said with a laugh.

She took his hand, and a sizzle of energy seemed to come through at the contact. Perhaps this was why everyone always insisted young women wear gloves. On the other hand, she suspected the thrill that thrummed through her at the briefest contact with him was something more unique to him.

She climbed over the wall, clutching hold of his hand. Her slippers slid over the rounded stones.

He frowned. "I have some spare boots in the carriage."

She grinned. "That would hardly do. Your feet are massive."

"Yes," he agreed. "Though I would say rather that yours are extraordinarily small."

"Extraordinarily is an unnecessary word."

"That is debatable."

He'd spoken so lightly to her and with such good humor, that she hadn't noticed that she'd clambered over the wall. He made it over as well and grinned.

She smoothed her dress. She was a country girl and wasn't supposed to be flummoxed at the sight of a field, even though she'd never approached them with such poor footwear before. She strode into the field, taking a dirt path a farmer had made. When they reached a gate, Hamish extended his hand and helped her over it. The rain started to drizzle down, but despite her rehearsed words to the contrary in London, she did not mind.

THE WHEEL WAS FIXED, and Hamish settled into the carriage. This time Georgiana climbed up after him, and he was happy for the company. They needed to press on to get to Gretna Green. With any luck, they would meet his brother before they reached Scotland.

Unfortunately, Callum didn't seem to want to be found. Georgiana and he stopped at every posting inn, and though

Hamish searched each inn's public spaces, he spotted neither Callum nor his intended bride. Upon being asked, no one recalled seeing them.

His brother's absence should have been frustrating, but relief prickled through him. He wasn't ready for a protracted argument about the merits of Callum marrying or not. Postponing that discussion was fine. After all, he didn't want to break Georgiana's heart if he won the argument, and he did not want to force any embarrassment or dishonor on the Butterworth family.

The journey to Scotland was proving vastly more pleasant than his journey away from it had been, and he suspected he could not explain that fact simply because Scotland was a far nicer destination.

He suspected it also had something—a great something—to do with Georgiana herself.

That fact was not something upon which to linger.

It was natural to feel some attraction to an unattached woman of a certain age with whom one was spending long periods of time, even if the woman in question was not Scottish, and even if she was the sister of one's brother's inappropriate fiancée.

Still, the lassie made him laugh like no other, and the tips of his lips were gaining more exercise than he'd thought possible.

"It's so pretty here," she mused.

"Is that why you sneaked onto the coach?" he teased.

She stiffened "No, of course not."

"I know," he said, his tone more serious. "And we will find your sister."

She nodded.

"So where have you been before?" he asked.

"Norfolk and London. And now Cambridgeshire."

"Do you miss Norfolk?"

She giggled. "I don't think any people from Norfolk would admit to missing it, though to be honest, it is pleasant. I do prefer the countryside, no matter how much grander and more imposing the buildings in London are. I can see that they're special, but I would still rather be outside, in nature. Façade admiration is really less enjoyable than flower admiration." She smiled. "Though you would probably disagree."

"Are you volunteering to drive this contraption, lassie, so I can sit inside and appreciate the architectural interior?"

She laughed.

"I'm going to get you to your sister," he said. "But if the gossips do find out about it—"

"Then it won't matter," she said firmly. "I will already have helped her."

"But what about your future?"

"Family is what is important. I couldn't let her think she was fleeing to happiness, when I knew that you were going after her to stop the wedding and remove that happiness from her."

"But I wasn't going after her. I didn't know she was planning to elope."

Georgiana gave a small sad smile. "That was my mistake. But my intention hasn't changed."

He nodded.

He'd thought her quite mad for her actions, but in truth, she'd only done what perhaps he would have done in a similar circumstance. They were both seeking to protect their siblings.

By hiding herself away in his carriage, she'd done what very few people might do, and the thought filled him with respect for her.

"Besides," she added, "I owed it to my parents."

"You're lucky to have them," he said. "I should like to know more about them."

"I'm sorry you don't have yours," she said gently.

He shrugged. "It's sad whenever anyone dies." He gave a laugh that somehow managed to sound jarring. "Callum and I were largely raised by nursemaids anyway, so when we had a guardian instead of a parent to instruct them, it didn't make much of a difference."

"Who was your guardian?"

"One of our neighbors. A distant relative." Hamish smiled. "Lord McIntyre. He and his wife raised us. Though they're both dead now too."

"McIntyre?" Georgiana asked. Her voice sounded faint. "As in Lady Isla McIntyre?"

Chapter Twenty

COMPREHENSION DAWNED on Georgiana.

Lord McIntyre was the father of Lady Isla McIntyre, the woman whom Callum was supposed to marry. She hadn't dwelled on Lord McIntyre, envisioning him as some crotchety neighbor pressuring Hamish to ensure his brother fulfilled some long-forgotten contract to whom Hamish was beholden for sheep grazing privilege or something equally unimportant when compared with true love and everlasting happiness.

She hadn't imagined Lord McIntyre had passed away, but that Hamish still felt honor-bound to see his desires fulfilled. Surely the man's pull must extend beyond that of a wealthy landowner to be appeased.

"Lord McIntyre did so much for Callum and me," Hamish said, and Georgiana averted her eyes.

"I see." She kept her voice steady and light, even as Hamish confirmed everything she did not desire to know.

"It was always Lord McIntyre's desire that Callum and Lady Isla should marry." Hamish's face darkened. Evidently, the reminder he might not fulfill his late guardian's desire saddened him. "He raised us, much more than our parents did when they were alive. He taught us horseback riding and chess. He taught us the names of plants and trees. He loved Scotland. He trusted Callum to provide for Lady Isla."

"What is Lady Isla like?" Georgiana asked, curious despite not wanting to know the answer.

Perhaps Hamish would rush home to his castle in the Highlands, away from the pettiness of the *ton*, and propose to her out of some familial duty or actual desire. She must be wonderful, perhaps even spectacular, if he thought she would make such a good match for his brother.

Or perhaps he loved Isla and simply wanted her to fulfill her dream?

The notion was overly romantic, and she shook her head. Perhaps she'd been reading too many Loretta Van Lochen novels lately, but she still felt tense.

"Lady Isla is everything my brother should marry," Hamish said.

The tension in Georgiana's spine did not ease.

"She's intelligent and pretty," Hamish added. "Lady Isla has long dark hair and green eyes that other men are always complimenting. I don't understand why Callum did not want to marry her. She impressed everyone, even other women, and you know how demanding their expectations can be."

Georgiana stiffened, but Hamish continued.

"I could understand if he was reluctant to marry her if there was anything unappealing about her, but there isn't," Hamish concluded.

Perhaps Hamish had not really thrown ice over her, but her limbs felt stiff, and she shuddered. She had an urge to laugh, as if to express wonder at his brother's foolishness, but when she attempted the action, it sounded jarring, even to her own ears.

It would have been far nicer to hear that Lady Isla was imperfect. Georgiana cursed herself for being uncharitable, but the fact remained. When the duke and Charlotte married—Georgiana had little doubt that they would—would the duke be forever musing about the life he could have had? With a woman who would have been an adept hostess, making excellent conversation with all the lairds and their families effortlessly? With a woman who would know what meals to serve and whom he would be confident that she could not pass any negative traits to her children?

Such as red hair.

Georgiana pushed away the thought. She was thinking about her sister's happiness. Her own hair color had nothing to do with it, naturally.

Georgiana had relatives who shared her hair color; it must be something common in her family.

Red hair did not seem common in other people's families.

She certainly was not imagining anything for herself.

After all, she abhorred Hamish. She'd told him so herself. But that seemed no longer true. She didn't despise him, and she might even miss him later.

She refused to contemplate the precise degree that she would miss him: the answer might be unpleasant.

"But I was asking you about your parents," Hamish said, perhaps sensing her discomfort, and Georgiana's reverie was broken. His voice seemed almost concerned, as if he might be aware he had upset her.

"Most people think my parents are eccentric," Georgiana said.

"I'm quite sure that in this case most people are correct."

Georgiana smiled. "Perhaps. The thing is that they're both intelligent. People don't think they are, because I couldn't identify each peer before I debuted, but mother knows so much about flowers and plants. She could have been a witch in the old days."

"Some people might still consider her one," Hamish observed.

"Excuse me?"

"The plants," Hamish said quickly. "I meant the plants."

"Oh." This time Georgiana giggled, and he soon joined her. "I thought you might have thought—"

"I didn't," Hamish said.

"Well," Georgiana said. "She's too fond of lace caps to ever switch to a pointed hat."

"That is quite sensible of her."

"You probably thought my family was mad."

"I did," Hamish agreed, and Georgiana stiffened.

He squeezed her hand, and she attempted to ignore the butterflies swirling inside her.

"But I thought that was quite nice," Hamish said.

"Madness appeals to you? You should have visited Bedlam while in London."

He chuckled. The sound was deep and appealing, reminding her of warm amaretto.

"I think it's nice that your family is so lively."

"My mother is lively."

He shrugged. "But your father was always present. That means something. Something nice."

Oh.

How odd that Hamish was the first to comment on it.

"How old were you when your parents passed away?" she asked.

"Seven."

"Tell me about them. What were they like? Do you remember much?"

His lips quirked into something resembling a smile, though Georgiana thought it closer to an expression of bravery.

"I shouldn't have asked," Georgiana said. "Forgive me."

He shook his head. "It's a good question. One I've asked myself many times. I remember other things from then. I remember my room, and how the light hit the curtains and the sound of the waves. I remember my third birthday and thinking time moved far too slowly. I remember some of the servants, and of course, I remember my brother."

She waited, then her heart clenched when she realized that was the end of his memories.

"I would have thought my parents would have made more of an impression on me than my curtains," Hamish remarked. "I'm not even interested in fabric, as my valet would be the first to attest."

"Perhaps you would have grown closer when you were older."

"Perhaps," Hamish said. "I hope so."

She frowned. "But I don't quite understand. Why do you worry about the estate? I thought you were maintaining it for the memory of your father, but he didn't even..." She stopped abruptly. She didn't want to tell him that his father had never made an impression on him as a child, a definite sign that he'd rarely visited Hamish as a child. There were some things one should never utter out loud, but Hamish seemed to understand her all the same.

Hamish, she realized, was always understanding everything. For a man with definite roguish tendencies, at least when it came to chamber trespassing, he was not a partygoer. He'd never once mentioned a gaming hell or told her of horse races in excruciating detail as had some other men in her acquaintance.

He cared for others. He looked out for others. He was admirable.

She mused over last night's agonies. She'd been so suspicious of him, but he hadn't harmed her.

"Why are you so eager for your brother to marry Lady Isla?"

"Must we discuss it?" he asked.

"I believe your schedule is free now. You do not even have to worry about driving. Or if perhaps walking requires your full concentration—"

"We can talk," he said abruptly. He raked his hand through his hair, obviously uncomfortable.

"Why is my sister not suitable enough for him? Is it because of Father's position? Or because we're English? Because you don't seem conceited all the time, but—"

"Not *all* the time?" He turned his head toward her and grinned. "I suppose I should take that as a compliment."

She was silent, willing him to share more.

"It's because of the castle," he said finally. "Montgomery Castle. My parents weren't gifted at money management. Apparently they saw the fact that they lived in a castle as an excuse to spend all manner of money, so much so that they had to mortgage the property that had been bequeathed them. I'm told they hosted the best balls on the isles. When they died, our guardian—"

"Lord McIntyre?"

He nodded. "The estate was never tied up with the title. When my parents died, Callum and I were still children, and so he bought the mortgage for us, with the understanding we could live in the castle when we were older as long as Callum married Lady Isla." He shrugged. "I suppose he wanted his daughter to be a duchess, but the offer was still kind."

"Not that kind."

"I just don't want Callum to regret his decision."

"You're trying to protect your brother."

"And future Montgomerys," Hamish added, and she smiled.

"It's easy to marry in Gretna Green," Hamish said. "They don't even require posting banns. God in heaven, they don't even require a minister. Everyone knows the blacksmith in Gretna Green has a nice side business, simply by virtue of his location over the Scottish border. But dissolving the marriage? That's difficult. And it can cause pain." He turned to her. "I don't need to remind you about Henry VIII."

"I'm aware."

"Good."

"I always did like history," she mused.

"Aye, then you do have some taste, lassie."

Chapter Twenty-one

THEY ARRIVED AT A POSTING inn. Hamish gave a quick check in the carriage park to see if his brother's carriage was there, but there was no sign. Perhaps they'd changed their transport, but none of the carts and wagons seemed probable methods of transportation for a duke.

Perhaps the duke was ahead of them. They'd wasted time when the wheel broke.

Hamish sighed. If he were on his own, he would simply hire a horse and gallop on ahead in pursuit of them. Georgiana probably could handle the coach on her own—she was clever, but he didn't want to abandon her to the whims of fate. What if another wheel broke? What if highwaymen attacked?

Tall hedges loomed on either side of the coach, and Hamish scanned the area, just in case any highwaymen decided to waylay them.

He shook his head. They would catch up with his brother at Gretna Green.

The sun had not yet set, and the stucco inn was swathed in pink and orange light.

"The Old Goblet?" Georgiana asked, staring at the sign.

"Likely an exaggeration," Hamish said optimistically, as he opened a wooden door and ducked underneath a low beam.

165

Patrons stared at them, and he was conscious of tension moving through Georgiana. Squeezing her hand seemed very appealing.

They would need to pretend to be married.

The thought caused him to smile, and he walked up to the proprietor. "My wife and I were hoping to spend the night here."

The proprietor, a man with bushy white hair, nodded. "Very well."

The other patrons looked curiously at them.

"And we'll need dinner too," Hamish said.

"I can send it to your room."

Hamish glanced at Georgiana.

They couldn't share a room.

They'd shared a coach last night, and he'd spent the time longing to claim her, even though he would have to deal with all the spatial challenges that the manufacturers had not accommodated for in their designs.

He'd never survive the night were they to be in the same room.

"We need two rooms," Hamish said.

The innkeeper frowned. "But you are married."

He cast a doubtful look on Georgiana which Hamish despised.

"Yes," Hamish said. "It's only—"

The innkeeper continued to look disapprovingly at them. "This 'ere is a right fine establishment. No riffraff. Or—er—ladies of the night."

"He snores," Georgiana said suddenly, and Hamish jerked his head in her direction. "Like a—"

"Thunderstorm," Hamish finished, smiling.

She grinned back and something that was very much like magic flickered between them.

"A really terrible thunderstorm," Georgiana said.

"I know there are not such bad thunderstorms in England," Hamish said. "You might not understand the significance of it."

"Think Scandinavia," Georgiana said. "Imagine if Thor himself decided to wage a bitter war from this man's nostrils."

The innkeeper widened his eyes and stared at Hamish's nose. "I-I wouldn't have guessed it."

"It's a hidden talent," Georgiana said benevolently.

"Perhaps—er—you would be most suited for the barn."

"I wouldn't want to disturb your horses," Hamish said. "They have to work in the morning to plow the ground."

"Oh." The innkeeper nodded. "That's very thoughtful of you."

"He has some good qualities," Georgiana said.

Hamish gave a modest shrug, even while feeling wilder than he had for years. He didn't make up lies to tell people, even the kind that misrepresented his ability to sleep without disturbing people.

"Two rooms then."

"Money is no hindrance," Hamish said magnanimously.

"Well then." The innkeeper said a number, and Hamish handed him some coin.

"Thank you."

"Perhaps one day you can improve," the innkeeper said gravely. "It is sad to see someone who struggles so with sleep when he's so young."

"Oh, I don't struggle with sleep," Hamish said.

"I have to throw a pail of water on him each morning to wake him up," Georgiana said in an explanatory tone.

"I suppose I could get that for you," the innkeeper said. He turned to his companion. "Can you—er—make sure this 'ere lady has a pail of water in the morning?"

The man nodded solemnly.

"That's right unconventional," the innkeeper said. "Perhaps I should try it on other guests." He leaned forward. "Some of them sleep rather too well after a long night, if you catch my drift. It never occurred to me to douse them in water, though."

"Oh, my wife is quite creative."

"It might only work on my husband," Georgiana said quickly, and the word "husband" sent a jolt through Hamish. "Most men might find the experience unpleasant."

The innkeeper gave a thoughtful nod.

"I'll—er—show you to your rooms." The innkeeper grabbed two keys. "You're just upstairs at the end of the hallway."

They took the keys and headed past stunned-looking patrons. Perhaps it hadn't been completely necessary for Georgiana to say he needed to have a bucket of water thrown over his head to wake him up. It probably also wasn't necessary to be quite so dramatic when referencing his snoring, especially since Hamish had always been proud he was not prone to snoring to begin with.

Hamish opened one room, and then the other. He peeked inside. "I believe this is—er—nicer. You'll want this one."

"Oh." Georgiana blinked. "If you're certain."

"It has paintings of flowers in it. The other one has birds."

"Neither are particularly architectural."

"But you'll prefer the flowers," he said, and she smiled back. *God in heaven.* The lassie had a magnificent smile.

Footsteps sounded behind them, and Hamish and Georgiana both jumped away, as if to expand the distance between them as much as possible.

"Oh, I am sorry," the innkeeper said. "I've just come with the bucket."

"THANK YOU," GEORGIANA squeaked.

"My pleasure." The innkeeper strode through the room, and some water sloshed from the bucket onto the floor. "My. What a romantic couple you are. Especially given your husband's snoring. That couldn't have been a pleasant surprise. Makes you quite the angel."

"Yes," Hamish agreed, and Georgiana's cheeks warmed.

Georgiana wasn't Hamish's wife, and he didn't think her an angel.

And yet, somehow the innkeeper's babbling made her body warm, and she considered that it might be quite nice if both those circumstances *were* true.

Of course, they weren't, and Georgiana forced the thought away.

They were friends. Nothing more. They were spending long hours on the coach, not in an effort to get to know each other, but so that Hamish might leave her with her sister and avoid anyone thinking he compromised her.

Her heart tightened, and she was grateful when the innkeeper left. She entered the bed quickly, not speaking to him, though her thoughts remained on him.

Chapter Twenty-two

THE NEXT MORNING TOOK them further into North Yorkshire, and the road became more difficult. Georgiana stared at the steep, soaring hills surrounding them. Goats had turned into their main source of company. The rain had formed deep rivulets, and the horses had to proceed more slowly, since they were hindered both by the uncomfortable angles of the slopes and the unevenness of the roads.

At the end of a day that had involved guiding the horses through perilous swerves and horse changes at each station, they arrived exhausted at a coaching inn. The stone walls, that looked as if they'd been there since the sixteenth century, seemed to portend good things, and Georgiana smiled when they stepped onto the stone-flagged floors. A roaring fire crackled in a large hearth, and Hamish approached the innkeeper.

"How can I help you?" the innkeeper asked with a broad smile. "Dinner? Lodging?"

"Aye," Hamish said. "Both of them."

The woman's cheery expression vanished, and Hamish stiffened.

Georgiana frowned. The woman had been friendly until she'd heard Hamish's Scottish accent.

"I might have one room," the innkeeper said, obviously reluctantly.

Perhaps she regretted announcing she had lodging moments before.

Hamish sent Georgiana a querying look, but Georgiana nodded. She was in no mood to make an excuse for why they couldn't share a room now. It seemed disloyal to state that she needed her own room because she couldn't abide to share one with Hamish, and of course she would hardly want to give this woman the impression that Hamish was traveling with an unwed woman.

"Do you have any extra bedding?" Hamish asked.

The innkeeper frowned. "I assure you, our bedding is sufficiently warm."

"I have confidence in the quality, but—"

"This is England, after all," the innkeeper interrupted. "You may be used to frigidness in the barren north, but I assure you in England we are quite comfortable."

Georgiana supposed the innkeeper might have a lax interpretation of the word comfort. The Moors seemed remote and hardly a holiday location for those seeking warmth coupled with relaxation, and she supposed the potential for the latter was limited when one was surrounded by unfriendly hosts.

"Is that so?" Hamish asked.

Georgiana had grown accustomed to the musical drawl of his words. His emphasis on the letter "R" seemed charming, but it was evident the man's accent brought no similar favorable reaction from the innkeeper.

"No doubt your bedding is tolerable," Georgiana said, hoping to lessen the tension ricocheting about the tavern and drawing attention from the tankard-clutching patrons, but unwilling to use a more enthusiastic word than tolerable to describe anything in this establishment.

"You're English." The innkeeper's eyes widened. "What are you doing with this man?" The innkeeper leaned forward and lowered her voice to a whisper that still somehow managed to be far too loud. "Don't you know 'e's Scottish?"

Georgiana shifted her feet over the wooden planks of the floor, unsettled by the woman's blatant prejudice and snobbery.

"I can tell by 'is accent," the woman continued, giving a proud smile.

"I didn't doubt your ability to tell," Georgiana said.

The woman beamed.

"Though I did wonder at the importance of that fact," Georgiana added, which caused the innkeeper to flash a much more disgruntled expression at her.

Hamish cleared his throat. "This is my—er—wife."

"And you require two sets of bedding?" The innkeeper asked again, then she paused. "But of course. You must be having an argument."

Georgiana gave Hamish an uneasy smile.

"I mean," the innkeeper continued, "It must be only natural, what with your different backgrounds."

"I'm very troublesome," Hamish said in a gentlemanly gesture.

"But not as troublesome as I am," Georgiana said quickly.

"I call her shrew for short," Hamish said.

"I suppose that meets the requirements in length for a nickname," the innkeeper said slowly.

"Indeed it does," Hamish said.

"And you wouldn't prefer two rooms?"

"Oh, her heart would ache too much if she were in a different room," Hamish said.

"Only because I would worry too much about his proclivity to shout out my name in the middle of the night," Georgiana replied. "The man is prone to missing me. Rather like a new kitten."

"She calls me kitten for short," Hamish said. "Even though it does not meet the requirements for shortness of length. She's rather less clever in that regard."

"Despite your Scottishness," the innkeeper said.

"Some Scots are quite clever with language," one of the patrons said. "Like that fellow."

"And Robert Burns," said another.

The innkeeper directed a sympathetic look at Georgiana. "You poor thing. But please do not worry, despite your husband's derogatory comments, I do consider 'kitten' to be a perfectly reasonable nickname. I only question that it might not suit his personality."

"Oh, he does *appear* strong and brave," Georgiana said.

"In that case," the innkeeper said firmly, "You will certainly get two sets of bedding. I'll even move a bed into your room."

"How splendid." Georgiana flashed a smile at Hamish, though the man did not seem nearly as amused.

"Did you need to give me that nickname?" Hamish whispered as they followed the innkeeper up the stairs.

"Did you see the looks she was giving you?" Georgiana asked. "I think they thought Scottish men frightening."

"Evidently not anymore," Hamish said mournfully.

"Oh, you'll survive," she said. "Besides, now you're getting a bed."

"You make it seem that I was going to be the one to sleep on the floor."

"Well, it wasn't going to be me!"

"You're the one who sneaked onto *my* coach."

Georgiana gave him an innocent shrug. "None of this would have happened if you hadn't tried to stop my sister's *wedding.*"

"It was a responsible action," Hamish grumbled. "You wouldn't understand."

The innkeeper led them up some rickety wooden steps to their chamber. Each creak of the steps seemed to sound an ominous tone to her heart with such efficiency that it would make the director of a music hall melodrama envious.

Because even though it might make sense to share a room here, and heavens, she'd learned her lesson about attempting to travel in the dark, the thought of actually being in an enclosed space with him was unsettling. This would differ from riding alongside on the perch for the driver, where they might comment on the scenery or simply enjoy the flutter of fresh air against their attire. This would even differ from when they'd slept side by side on the stiff seats inside the coach. Beds had different connotations.

The innkeeper marched quickly, as if unwilling to waste any time with them.

"You can go downstairs to grab your grub when you're ready," the innkeeper said. "I won't bring it for you."

"That's fine," Georgiana said hastily.

The innkeeper nodded and pushed open the door to a room. She jerked her thumb in the room's direction, then turned to go downstairs, muttering about foreigners.

Georgiana entered the room, conscious of Hamish behind her.

She had been right not to desire to share a room before. Perhaps she'd shared a room with her sister in their parents' home in Norfolk, but this in no manner compared.

The man's presence dominated the room, despite the generous square footage the posting inn had allotted for it.

Georgiana forced her attention on her new surroundings. Perhaps musing on the pleasant paintings of windmills and hay stacks that dotted the room would distract her from him.

He was standing, and his towering stature was unmistakable, emphasized by the medieval timbers that lined the ceiling.

"They gave us a nice room," she said, but he merely arched an eyebrow.

Heat rushed to her cheeks.

Of course.

The man's brother was a duke.

Hamish wouldn't have spent his childhood sharing a room with his brother. He would have had his own room. His home wouldn't have had a thatched roof: it would have been a castle with towers, bartizans, crenellations, and perhaps even a dungeon where he could threaten to lock up any tiresome cousins. He wouldn't have played in a garden, careful to not trample over the vegetables or pierce himself with the thorny rose stems. He would have had an entire estate on which to roam about.

"This is probably too old-fashioned for you." She gave a forced laugh, conscious that her cheeks were growing warmer, not cooler.

His eyes widened. "I don't mind old-fashioned things."

"Truly?"

He nodded. "Why would you think that?"

"I mean, you're the brother of a duke. The son of a duke. The cousin of..."

"A marquess," he finished for her, and she smiled.

"Yes," she said. "I mean you must be accustomed to a certain level of elegance, and perhaps this room, which I consider nice, doesn't quite meet those standards. And now I'm rambling." She clamped her mouth shut. "I-I should stop talking. I must be tired."

"We should sleep," he said.

"Yes," she agreed quickly, even though she'd never felt more awake. Sleep was an impossibility when her heart hammered and her nerves fluttered.

Her hands quivered, and she smoothed her dress, as if a wrinkle were unsettling her and not the fact that they were alone in a room.

"You should change from it," Hamish said. "That can't be comfortable."

It wasn't.

The buttons and laces made changing from the dress on her own a daunting task.

"It's—"

Comprehension seemed to dawn on Hamish. "I should have realized. I can help you."

Hamish closed the distance between them, and Georgiana's heart leapt, as if it had decided to dance a cotillion right inside her chest.

She turned around quickly. No need for him to see her cheeks flush. The idea was perhaps imperfect, for in the next moment his hands were upon the back of her dress.

She'd never longed for a linen dress more. The sensation of Hamish's fingers brushing against her back shouldn't remind her of fire. He undid her dress, and her shoulders relaxed, glad to be rid of the fabric.

"You're smiling," Hamish said.

"I was thinking of how much I once longed to have this dress. I suppose things change."

"Yes," Hamish said, and something about his expression made her shiver.

He withdrew his gaze. "Are you comfortable now? Or would you like me to—er—"

His gaze dropped to below her face, and she was aware she was only standing in her shift.

"No," she said quickly. "You needn't remove it."

His cheeks darkened. "Naturally. But perhaps I should loosen your laces."

Oh.

Of course the man was unlikely to want her to sleep with nothing at all on.

"Perhaps loosening them would be nice," she acquiesced, and he nodded. Even though she should be accustomed to his touch on her back, her skin still prickled at his touch, evidently finding his movements of great interest. When they lay to sleep, her heart still thrummed.

Chapter Twenty-three

THE NEXT DAY, THE COACH rumbled over medieval cobblestones, and they entered Carlisle. The town had crept up on Hamish, appearing out of the desolate landscape. Evidently, Georgiana was conscious of the influx of people. She shivered and leaned back against the seat of the coach.

Hamish's lips twitched. "They won't be able to tell that we're not married, despite their intelligence."

"They might be able to recognize me," Georgiana said. "Or you."

"Doubtful." Hamish pressed his lips together in a firm line, calculating the likelihood that someone, in a thick cluster of people, might be familiar with either of them. He pulled the coach over. "Get inside."

Georgiana nodded and clambered down the steps. She moved quickly but perhaps not quickly enough.

"Lord Hamish Montgomery!" A voice soared behind them. "Is that you?"

"Must be someone else," Hamish said quickly.

The voice laughed. "I'd recognize that voice anywhere. It's Wolfe. Don't tell me you've forgotten."

"Of course not," Hamish relented. He forced a smile on his face and lied. "How wonderful to see you."

His mind raced. This was Lady Isla's brother. The man was not only a member of the *ton,* who could destroy Georgiana's reputation, he was also a man who would bear a very strong grudge against her family.

He swallowed hard.

This was...*not* wonderful.

God in heaven.

Of all the people in all of England to run into, he had to have run into Wolfe. It didn't help in the slightest that Wolfe knew him well. The man would find it dashed suspicious to see Hamish on this side of the border. Wolfe knew that Hamish held even the southern portions of Scotland in disdain, seeing them as ineffectual defenses against the English.

Normally, happening upon Wolfe would definitely be considered pleasant. The man was likely to find Hamish's lack of a smile upon seeing him as belonging to the odder parts of his day.

Hamish glanced at Georgiana. She hadn't made it inside yet, and his heart sank.

"It's been a while," Wolfe said, not missing any time before casting a piercing glare at him. Hamish shifted his legs. Wolfe's sister was much more pleasant.

At any moment Wolfe would probably ask why he was in England and whom he was traveling with. Neither question was one Hamish had any desire to answer.

"Your hair has grown bushier," Hamish said.

"You could have mentioned that my chest has grown broader," Wolfe grumbled. "It *has* been awhile."

"I thought I would find you in a place like London."

"Don't tell me *you* went to London." Wolfe's eyes rounded, and he looked toward Georgiana. "And who is this?"

GEORGIANA'S HEART THUDDED in her chest. She realized how lucky they'd been before to not meet anyone. And to meet this particular person, someone Hamish clearly did not desire to see? Georgiana shuddered.

"It's—er—" Hamish's face reddened.

They hadn't agreed on other names. The last thing she needed was for him to announce her real name. She needed to have some hope that she hadn't thoroughly ruined her reputation beyond absolute repair.

"My name is—er—Garnet Valentina."

Hamish's eyes widened. Perhaps she needn't have chosen a name of such eccentricity.

"Garnet." Wolfe gave a contemplative smile. "What a lovely name. Most *seductive*."

Perhaps the name was ridiculous.

Hamish frowned. "Yes. Her parents noted her hair color upon her—er—entry into the world."

Hamish's voice was icy, and Georgiana frowned. He needn't be so upset at her name choice. He hadn't been able to offer a better one, and he'd had the chance.

"I didn't know Hamish was in the practice of driving about with such beautiful women," Wolfe said.

"Hamish is a secretive man."

"Really? Most people would consider him dull."

Indignity trickled through Georgiana, and she noted that Hamish's reliably sun-kissed skin had a novel rosy tint.

"I don't consider him dull." She tossed her hair and did her best to give a regal glower.

Apparently regal glowers were expressions she was able to convey, for Wolfe looked somewhat chastened.

If he felt uncomfortable, Georgiana did not regret it. The man couldn't expect to insult Hamish. Hamish might spend time going over the books of his family's estate, but that was not something to deride. The man's passion wasn't in mathematics, and if it were, she doubted he would find checking that the rows of columns matched in his ledger stimulating. No, Hamish's passion was for architecture.

"So who are you?" Wolfe turned to her. "Because I've met Hamish's relatives. And you're not one of them."

"I'm not related to Lord Hamish," she said.

Wolfe's eyes rounded. "Not at all?"

Hamish's expression seemed to belong to the horror-struck variety, and Georgiana regretted that she'd been quite so decisive.

Perhaps it would have been fine if Wolfe had thought that Hamish had a younger cousin, perhaps educated at one of the atrocious finishing schools to account for her English accent.

But on the other hand... She was Garnet Valentina. Not Georgiana Butterworth from Norwich, Norfolk. Not a woman to be pitied to have grown up far from the *ton*'s strongholds between Kent and Hampshire, and far from the supposedly romantic moors of Yorkshire or Dartmoor that seemed to intrigue people, even though Georgiana was quite certain that Norfolk had every advantage since it did not possess impossibly steep slopes and was not ridden with marshy bogs in which people could drown.

She moved the tartan blanket lower. The man's gaze followed it to her bosom but she resisted the urge to long for a fichu or to cover it immediately. Garnet Valentina wouldn't do such a thing. If the man suspected that she were a woman of the *ton*, well he would be asking everyone if they knew any red-headed women of a certain age and tell about how he'd seen her traveling alone in Durham.

The only thing she could do was to continue with her ruse.

"I am afraid we are in a rush." She fluttered her eyelashes and lowered her voice so it had a seductive edge. "Hamish gets dreadfully impatient."

"Does he?" Wolfe's lips quirked. "I do have accommodation should you require it."

"Dearest?" Georgiana glanced at Hamish. "What do you think?"

"Absolutely not," Hamish growled.

"We desire privacy," Georgiana said.

"Ah." The word was curt, but Wolfe rolled his gaze down Georgiana's figure. She had the impression he was taking her in as effectively as the best seamstress. "I can understand that. Well, it was a pleasure to meet you, Miss Valentina."

"The pleasure is mine, Mr. Wolfe." She curtsied, hoping that was an action for ladies of the night.

The man smiled again. "Most men call me Lord McIntyre. But Wolfe will do very well for you."

She stiffened.

"That is an extraordinary name." Georgiana's voice trembled.

"Befitting of an extraordinary man," Wolfe said smugly.

Hamish was definitely glowering now, and the thought brought her some amusement.

"But there are not many Valentinas here," Wolfe said.

"I'm not from here," she said.

"Well, that much is obvious." Wolfe smiled. "Valentina sounds Spanish, but Garnet..."

Georgiana thought quickly. "My father was a pirate. And my mother's family. She was from Cornwall."

"The red hair," Wolfe said.

Georgiana nodded, though she didn't like that people tended to think that red hair was the exclusive property of Cornwall. Her hair was auburn, and she'd lived most of her life quite comfortably in Norfolk, even if it had perhaps been not without frustrations that the color was rare. Her mother had washed it in buttermilk, but the color had never changed.

"And how did you meet dear Hamish?" Wolfe asked, his dark eyes glowing.

"London. At an—er—very exclusive place."

He turned to Hamish. "You go to London now? How exciting. What will become of the estate?"

"I was on important estate business." Hamish's frown deepened.

"Ah," Wolfe said, stifling a yawn. "How wonderful."

Georgiana had the impression Wolfe didn't find Hamish's dedication to his family the least bit appealing, and she frowned.

"Hamish is a most exciting man," she said. "You must not know him very well."

Wolfe appeared chastened. "I suppose I do not know him as well as his...mistress." He tilted his head. "Are you certain you're not up for a proper visit?"

"Absolutely not." Hamish dragged Georgiana back onto the driver's seat of the coach, and her heart raced at the ease with which he pulled her up. He grabbed the reins and urged the horses forward.

"See?" Georgiana called back to Wolfe. "Quite exciting!"

Wolfe's lips turned into a wide grin, and he waved.

Hamish urged the horses into a trot, and soon they sped through Durham and back into the comfort and seclusion of the countryside.

Chapter Twenty-four

THE BUILDINGS FLEW by in a delightful blur. If Wolfe was in the company of any friends whom Hamish knew, Hamish was driving far too quickly to ascertain.

"You shouldn't have said that," Hamish said.

"I know. I was upset."

"Garnet Valentina." Hamish's voice was rich with amusement.

Georgiana flushed. "It was the first name I could think of."

"It's not a name that springs easily to my mind."

Georgiana squared her shoulders. "That's because you weren't just reading *The Dashing Man and the Spanish Princess*. Miss Valentina is the heroine of that story."

"Ah..." Hamish smiled, but Georgiana was hesitant, as if expecting malice to appear in his eyes.

None did.

"That was clever," Hamish said.

"Oh?"

"Wolfe completely believed your pirate past. You were most seductive. An utter siren. Very pirate appropriate."

"You're teasing me," Georgiana said.

People didn't confuse her with seductive sirens. She was a Butterworth, the child of a long string of vicars. They expected her to sing hymns and arrange flowers. Sirens weren't assumed to have knowledge of gardening. Any flowers they had were brought by suitors and not planted beside sensible vegetable patches.

She'd never lied like that. Perhaps she'd let Hamish believe she was her younger sister, but she never would have introduced the idea.

And yet, today, she'd concocted a new persona. Her lips moved upward. She supposed she'd had a bit of help from Loretta Van Lochen.

Hamish directed the horses into a posting inn, then he helped her from the coach. She touched his hand, and warmth shot through her as he guided her down the steps. The man affected her effortlessly. She'd noticed the handsome manner in which Lord McIntyre had styled his hair and the fashionable cut of his attire, but it was Hamish who caused her heart to quicken. When she reached the cobblestones, she glanced up, only to find that she was far too near him. His cravat was not supposed to brush against her nose, and she squeezed her eyes shut.

Her heart wasn't supposed to quicken, and her breath wasn't supposed to either. It was a shame that the first time she'd been alone with a man, it had been to one such as Hamish. It would be far more convenient if they'd despised each other.

Georgiana did her best to think about things she abhorred about Hamish. Unfortunately, all the things that she'd most hated about him, she now understood. Perhaps he'd broken into her room and waved coin before her eyes, but he'd been trying to act best for both his brother and the woman he'd thought had inappropriately claimed him. He hadn't tried to threaten his brother's bride; he'd offered to set her up to live independently for the rest of her life. Other men would not be so generous.

"I'm not a seductress." She laughed, conscious that her voice sounded too high pitched.

Hamish didn't smile.

Instead, his eyes darkened. "I wouldn't be too certain."

His voice sounded hoarse, almost husky, and she glanced up.

"You must have thought me ridiculous," she said.

"I didn't." Hamish's eyes were serious. "Indeed you're the most seductive woman I've ever come across."

Memories of that kiss, that wonderful, delightful kiss, thrummed through her, and her heart squeezed.

Hamish had spent time with her.

He'd traveled with her.

They'd made conversation, not guided by the interests of her mother and convention, which tended to be heavy on musings over the weather and the preferred method of drinking tea.

She averted her eyes.

He was being polite.

It was an instinct that shouldn't surprise her. She knew now he was dutiful, even if his actions might seem absurd. Men were always complimenting women's appearances, as if remarking on a shade of locks or eye color could be the same as actual conversation.

And yet his voice did sound huskier than before.

Though, then again, *her* voice varied as well. Perhaps it was the weather. Perhaps the thick floral fragrance in the air was irritating their throats, and Georgiana was considering that he might actually like her even though there was a scientific, and decidedly unromantic reason for the lowering of his voice.

His gaze roamed her features. "That hair—"

"Is too red," Georgiana finished.

"No," he said firmly. "It's vibrant. Like a flame."

The man's gaze remained intense.

Smoldering.

The space between them was narrow, and for a wild moment she thought Hamish might close the gap even farther. Wind fluttered against her dress, and she shivered.

She was unsure whether she'd trembled because of the frigid temperature or because of Hamish's presence, but Hamish's expression immediately changed.

"Let's get you inside." He headed for the inn. People sat outside, gazing at them curiously, and warmth flooded Georgiana's cheeks.

Hamish soon arranged for a room. The innkeeper gave them the key and pointed to a rickety staircase.

One room.

"We must be practically in Gretna Green," Hamish said.

Georgiana didn't question why he desired to spend the night here. It *would* be dark soon. Perhaps Gretna Green accommodations were limited. Likely he was being sensible in desiring to wait.

And yet...

Was he perhaps reluctant to end their time traveling?

The thought should have been absurd, but she couldn't push it away.

Hamish pushed the key in the lock and turned it. They entered a dark room.

Tension seemed to swirl between them, and her heart raced. "It's a nice room."

"I thought you would wait until you could see the room before you praised it."

It was dark.

Warmth crept over Georgiana's neck. "I—I"

"You're polite," Hamish said, and amusement rang in his baritone voice.

Something sounded in the dark, and then candlelight flickered over the room, casting golden rays about. "It went out earlier."

"Oh," Georgiana said. "That was silly of me."

"You're not silly." He leaned close, and something like desire shone in his eyes.

Something was about to happen.

Georgiana knew she should make an excuse to leave the room. She should step away and chatter about something the man had no interest in, like table settings or napkin folding trends. That was the sort of thing her mother and every governess she ever had would recommend.

And yet there was nowhere she would rather be. And even though this moment seemed rife with potential uncertainty, Georgiana remained. The man might as well have conjured her to stone: moving was unthinkable.

Hamish stretched his hand toward her and then ran his fingers through her hair. A thrill thrummed through Georgiana, tumbling straight to her toes, even though hair touching should have absolutely nothing to do with nerve endings in feet.

Hamish's hands were doing intriguing things, moving from her locks to her dress. Her skin prickled, but in a manner so novel, so full of pleasure, that she could only stare at him, bewildered.

It didn't seem possible that a hand might wield such power, and yet the only thought that occupied her was where it might stray next.

He coursed his fingers over her dress, veering toward her bosom. Her body ached for him, and in the next moment he brushed his lips against hers.

They kissed.

It was more tentative than the last time they'd kissed.

It meant more.

He pushed her against the wall, and the timber beams pressed against her spine. The action should have felt uncomfortable. Flora would have reminded her to take care of the mesh overlay on her dress, but the only thing that concerned Georgiana was the feel and taste of Hamish's lips.

Delight soared through her. Chocolate and meringues were poor sources of pleasure when compared to the simple feel of his arms about her. She arched her head up, taking in his towering presence. His shoulders began where her eyes were placed, and she took in the dark strands of his hair and the man's emerald eyes.

"I desire you," Hamish growled.

Georgiana's heartbeat quickened. "Because I said I was Miss Valentina?"

The words were clumsy, and she waited for the man to laugh, but instead he tilted her chin, holding it between his fingers. "No. You're better. You're *you*."

She must have appeared confused, for he continued. "I've never met a braver lassie. You're clever and quick thinking—"

"And I get myself into trouble," she interjected.

This time he did smile. "I believe you're not the only troublemaker in this room."

"Are you referring to sneaking into my room?"

"I did think you were your sister. But I'm very glad I was wrong."

His eyes twinkled, and despite all the impropriety, she found herself smiling back.

"You're loyal," he added solemnly. "Perhaps you get yourself into some trouble, but it's only to protect others. And I can't see that as a bad thing."

No one had ever viewed her impulsivity in this light before. She was quiet as he continued to catalogue her advantages, even though no one, ever, took the time to praise her.

"And of course," he said. "You're beautiful."

"You mustn't be polite."

"I'll remember that next time I'm confronted with a door when I walk with you."

Her lips twitched. She had no doubt that Hamish would continue to do the right thing and open it for her.

He continued to look at her solemnly. "Your skin is so soft, and your eyes are a vivid shade of brown."

She decided not to remind him that people seldom raptured about skin that contained freckles and that brown was not a color that most people referred to as vivid. "Dull" and "a shame" were the phrases her relatives had most commonly used when referring to them. Words were things she'd once been able to form, but her throat dried, and speaking was an elaborate process impossible to contemplate.

Life consisted only of Hamish and her.

The world had become narrower and yet richer than she'd ever been able to imagine.

"I want to be with you," Hamish said. "I want to—"

"Yes," Georgiana said quickly.

He paused. "Are you certain?"

Georgiana knew the correct answer was no. She was from the country. She'd had some independence. One didn't spend one's whole life being warned against doing something and then never wonder what that thing entailed. And yet, soon they would arrive in Gretna Green, and she would join her sister's protection, hopefully now imbued with all the dignity of a married woman. How could Georgiana return to her quiet life now? Would her parents be grateful that at least one daughter had married and whisk her away to the Norfolk countryside? A fate of organizing her father's library and taking over household duties from her mother had seemed a relief sometime after the end of her second season. She'd grown tired of the assessing looks from the men she was introduced to during the season. She'd been dismissed as too bold, too lively, without the virtues of peaches-and-cream skin, flaxen hair, and blue eyes from which might alternatively conjure similes about cerulean skies or azure oceans, depending on their preference.

If her life was to return to the calm of Norfolk, did she want to leave without experiencing everything life had to offer? Being proper wasn't what had compelled her to board Hamish's coach in, albeit mistaken, pursuit of her sister. Being proper was something that other people advocated, and something that she suspected was of greater convenience to themselves. Being proper would be a possibility tomorrow once she caught up with her sister. It was not a necessity for tonight.

"I want...everything," she murmured.

His face lit up, and she hadn't realized how constrained, how on edge, he must have been.

He pulled her into his arms, but this time, he lifted her and carried her toward the bed. This time she didn't struggle. This time she only marveled at his strength, and she felt secure in his arms.

"Beds," he declared, "Are a marvelous invention."

"Indeed?" she breathed.

"Aye," he said solemnly. "Particularly on this sort of occasion."

"And what sort of occasion is that?" she asked, her voice somewhat faint.

"The very best sort." He placed her on the bed, and she sank against the cool bedspread. The quilted texture prickled her skin, but in the next moment Hamish lay down beside her, drawing her closer to him.

She might desire this, but this was still new, and uncertainty rippled through her.

It wouldn't do for Hamish to think she was being anything except practical. He might admire her, but he didn't want to be saddled with a wife, particularly one of the English variety, a strain of British that compelled him to leave no insult unused.

The single tallow candle flickered light about the room, and she angled her head away from it, lest she gaze at Hamish in unbridled adoration, and he feel honor-bound to halt their delightful explorations of flesh.

No, it was far better for him to think her merely curious, the sort of thing that had compelled Her Grace, the Duchess of Alfriston, to seek a career in archeology and which had made Miss Louisa Carmichael, the duchess's sister-in-law, study everything she could about marine life. Tonight he should think himself a replacement for a book.

But then he kissed her, and when he lifted his head and smoothed her hair from her face, his gaze seemed to be one of such open wonder, that Georgiana decided that feigning coolness was an unnecessary task when there were so many pleasurable ones: such as kissing every inch of the man's flesh.

The fire and candlelight flickered golden light over Hamish's skin, and she inhaled his manly scent. She'd grown accustomed to that peculiar mix of cedar and cotton, but now with their bodies pressed together, she allowed herself to succumb to the novel sensation.

Chapter Twenty-five

SHE WAS MAGNIFICENT.

Poets could compose sonnets about the color of her hair and her large dark eyes.

Hamish was no poet. There was one thing he wanted to do: ravish her.

He had no time for musings. It was simply obvious that no loch, no meadow, no hilltop—no matter the clearness of any water, the composition and variety of any flowers, and the intriguing slope of any incline—could compete with the simple image of her on the bed beneath him.

Because the simple fact was that he adored her. In fact, Hamish was quite certain there was a stronger word that expressed how he felt about her: *love*.

It was a word he hadn't used with anyone before, but he mused over its significance as their lips danced and swayed as they kissed.

He would marry her.

It didn't matter if they found Georgiana's sister or not. It didn't matter if Georgiana's sister was already a duchess and could craft the loftiest, most believable excuse for Georgiana.

He still wanted to marry her. Georgiana had brought everything wonderful into his life, and there was no way he would deposit her at Gretna Green into her sister's care, as if nothing in the world had changed.

"You're smiling," Georgiana breathed.

"I have you."

The sentence made her moan, and Hamish concentrated on making more lovely moans come from her throat. She tasted like vanilla, and his nostrils flared. Her skin was soft, some delicious combination of silk and velvet, and he tore his lips from hers and pressed kisses against her long elegant neck, her collar bone, all the places of such beauty that he sought to memorize them for all time, as if the action of kissing them might imprint them on his mind.

Then he smiled.

He wouldn't need to memorize anything. He intended to have her here, by his side, for the rest of their lives.

Right now he faced a more immediate problem: her dress.

The gown was beautiful of course, no matter how he teased her. It was feminine. Something about the gauzy overlay and the flowers sewn on it was charming, even if she wouldn't have looked entirely out of place on one of the Regent's elaborate desserts at the pavilion in Brighton. But the dress was entirely too constrained, and it was absolutely necessary to remove her from it. *Immediately.* He wanted Georgiana, and he wanted her naked, without even the finest textures to separate them.

He traced the curve of one breast with his hand, indulging in the soft sensation of her luscious form. He wanted to bury himself in her bosom, to never let her go, but for now, he turned her over, even though the action seemed absurd. Not seeing her face seemed a vast disadvantage to seeing her face, but he stared at the column of buttons on her back and resisted the urge to curse.

He'd always prided himself on the large size of his hands, but now they seemed an impediment. He moved his fingers slowly over her back. The mesh overlay felt suddenly impossibly fragile, and the frills and ribbons on the top of her gown seemed like an unwanted deterrent. Each flounce and ribbon seemed as forbidding as one of Bonaparte's finest forts.

He moved valiantly, undoing each ribbon. It wasn't the first time he'd removed a woman's dress, but it was the first time that the action seemed imbued with such urgency. There seemed something sacred in the action, and as he slid the dress over her hips, a sense of almost trepidation moved through him.

Because no matter the carnal pleasure he took in the act itself, no matter the baseness of the sensation of flesh against flesh, sweat merging with sweat, the fact was that Georgiana mattered.

He turned her over, staring into her beautiful brown eyes. "Are you sure you want to do this?"

She tensed beneath him, and for a horrifying moment Hamish thought that she would confess that she had no such desire.

"Y-Yes," she stammered. "I mean... If you still desire—"

"Naturally." He enveloped her once again in an embrace. "A thousand times yes."

The women he'd seen in Edinburgh, bored wives eager to invite young men into their beds, seeing the action as diverting as hat shopping or selecting ribbons, might have laughed at his question.

Georgiana was different. If she desired to bed him, it was not out of a sense of anger that gossipmongers were reporting that her husband was frolicking with one of her friends. She was not distracting herself because the maids always seemed nervous in her husband's presence or because she was never able to retain a governess to stay long with her children. She was not a woman who simply saw Hamish as capable of fulfilling pleasures that her husband had long ago abandoned or had never been able to adequately meet. Perhaps their age, oddities of appearance or demeanor had never drawn their wives to them, at least not as much as their titles, wealth and the encouragement of the women's parents.

Hamish removed Georgiana's dress, folding the delicate gown with reverence and placing it on a nearby chair. The bed sank as he moved back, tumbling him closer to her, and he once again succumbed to kisses. Kissing had always seemed perfectly pleasant, but the act now seemed imbued with greater significance and far greater pleasure.

Her shift would need to come off. The long linen fabric looked as complex to remove as any dress, especially given the woman's tightly drawn stays that further enclosed her chest, even as it managed to arrange her bosom in a particularly alluring manner. The coarse tightly woven fabric of her stays was rough against his hands, and he yearned to touch her skin. It didn't matter in the least how daintily tied the ribbons were, or how fetching and becoming the light pink color of her stays looked against her skin.

She'd made his heart lurch from the moment he first saw her, and it hadn't simply been from seeing her in her night rail.

He undid the tightly pulled stays, wondering how the woman could have worn something so obviously uncomfortable for so long without complaint. He removed the garment slowly. His hands shook, even though his hands never shook.

Georgiana assessed him. "Do you intend to keep your tailcoat on?"

"No," he said, his voice suddenly hoarse.

She smiled. "Then I believe you will need to remove it."

He nodded, and in the next moment, her hands were on his. She brushed her fingers against the fabric, and he remembered that she'd worn it herself. He slid the tailcoat off.

This time he did not bother folding it.

It could remain utterly wrinkled for the rest of the trip, and he did not care. If it meant he had a moment more of kissing her, then it was worth it.

His sleeves billowed, unconstrained by his coat. Georgiana was more interested in his waistcoat, or at least, the process of removing it. Her fingers were gentle but not without efficiency. He decided to get to work on his cravat and unwound the linen fabric. Before long his chest was bare, and Georgiana traced his muscles with her fingers. Her silky touch managed to send fire jolting through his body, and he ached to be inside her. His muscles flexed at her touch, and her cheeks pinkened.

"Continue," he said.

"It's so hard," she said.

He smirked, and her blush deepened.

"And your body is delightfully soft," he said.

She bit her bottom lip, and he feathered kisses over her face. He pulled the pins from her hair, so her luscious locks fell to her pillow. He ran his fingers through her hair, moving the satiny strands to her waist.

"You're glorious," he said. "Utterly glorious."

She wrapped her arms around him, as if to clasp him more tightly to her, as if she agreed that any space between them was to be avoided. She combed his hair with her fingers and wrapped her ankles around his.

For some strange reason Hamish felt he belonged to her every bit as much as she belonged to him.

It was sentimental nonsense of course. Utter balderdash, the sort of thought that would make him roll his eyes if another man expressed it, and yet, here he was, in Georgiana's arms, thinking the thought himself.

He was hers.

He wanted to pleasure her.

She was his queen.

Evidence of his desire arched against her. He craved her, and the urge to raise her shift and slide into bliss thrummed through him.

He resisted the temptation. This was about Georgiana.

The shift didn't come off. Kissing was becoming far too interesting, and separating from her again to tear off further garments seemed like an inefficient use of time. Her skin was warm against his, and he smiled, knowing that the fire that blazed through him was not imaginary.

He craved her, and she, despite her propriety, gave every evidence of craving him.

He cupped her breast, and even through her shift, he felt her quiver beneath him. Her cheeks darkened, and her eyes widened as she gave a sudden moan. She hooked her ankles more tightly around him, as if realizing that it was his body that could bring her relief. Beads of sweat lined her brow, and he wiped them away with his hand.

It didn't matter that he was the brother without a title, the brother who had been just a bit too late. It didn't matter that he didn't spend his time in gaming hells and that, unlike his cousin Lord Rockport, he didn't top lists of rogues. He spent too little time in high society for women to decide whether to adore or avoid him.

"If you were to seduce me," Georgiana asked, "Would you be wearing pantaloons?"

He grinned. "Absolutely not."

"Ah." She lay back onto the bed, and her eyes glimmered. "Perhaps you should demonstrate."

He tore his pantaloons off. His valet would have been impressed by his speed, and Hamish flung the pantaloons in the general direction of the door. The one good thing about staying in a posting inn would be that there would be no maid to come to light a fire in the hearth who might be shocked by his behavior.

Georgiana had removed her gaze from Hamish's face, and it was now pointed directly at the evidence of his desire.

Her eyes were wider than before. "That is—"

"Massive. Magnificent. Mighty." Hamish grinned. "I want to spare you the bother of making conversation."

Her eyes sparkled. "Is that how you seduce women?"

It wasn't, he realized. Those situations had been formal in their own way, comprised of each party giving a series of appropriate compliments as they entered each stage of the act. He'd already spent more time with Georgiana than he had with any other woman, and somewhere along the way he'd found an easy comfort with her.

The ropes sank between them, tumbling her closer to him, and she laughed.

"That shift is going to have to come off," he growled.

"That shift is the only item keeping me proper."

"Then I despise it," he said, directing a glower at the coarse linen.

She laughed. "Then I think you'll have to remove it."

"I will." Hamish clutched both sides of the bottom of her shift and pulled it over her head. He'd already removed her stays, and he removed the shift without a great deal of effort.

And then he was silent.

Transfixed.

Georgiana was still in his arms, but this time she was utterly naked. His pulse quickened. His desire throbbed, jutting into her soft flesh.

He drank her in. Imbibed her. She surpassed the finest wine, the finest whisky. Her skin was luminescent, save for the auburn curls on her intimate part. Her waist was slimmer than he'd imagined, fragile in his arms, though her hips splayed in a delightful, rounded manner. Her bosom was perched high, and he circled her rosebuds with his fingers, tracing the manner it pebbled against his hand.

"You've gone silent," Georgiana said, and her long lashes fluttered up.

Hamish blinked and pulled her onto his lap.

Perhaps silence was not the sort of thing a woman wanted in bed.

His throat was dry, and he willed his mouth to speak, even though speech seemed like an overly complex act in the circumstances.

"You are utterly beautiful," he said finally, conscious that his voice was hoarse. "You're a queen. A goddess. A—"

"You can call me goddess," Georgiana said, rolling off his lap and displaying a wonderfully pert bottom.

Every part of Hamish tightened, and the room was suddenly much, much hotter than it had been moments before.

The woman didn't understand what that position was doing for her body as she stretched, and with a groan he lowered himself over her.

Their lips met, and bliss ensued.

Her skin tasted like the ocean, and their legs tangled together. They kissed, and life was magnificent. Any initial timidity from her had vanished, as if her tongue knew just what to do to his, as if her lips were meant for him and him alone, and as if her arms knew just how to squeeze, just how to rub, just how to—

He tore himself from her, his heart beating wildly.

"Hamish?" she asked.

"Stop."

"But—"

"Otherwise this is going to end." He swallowed hard, conscious he wasn't quite explaining things.

She settled back down on the bed, and Hamish placed his knees between hers and lowered himself over her, positioning himself at her entrance.

She moved her arms around him, hugging him against her.

"I don't want to crush you."

"I'm strong."

In the next moment she was pulling him even more tightly to her, as if their heartbeats might send each other some code.

And then he pushed forward into her. He moved gently, meeting with resistance, and he rested against her. She was wet. Warm. Everything he craved.

She tangled her fingers in his hair and kissed him.

He obliged.

They kissed for hours, or perhaps just minutes. He'd always prided himself on his sense of time, but his understanding of even the most basic principles vanished. She rocked against him, unconsciously, and he pushed further.

He was inside her.

Nothing rivaled this pleasure. Her eyes were wide, as if surprised.

He stroked her cheek. "Are you in pain?"

She shook her head, but he slowed inside her all the same and continued to feather kisses over her.

And then at some point she tightened about him. His speed quickened, and his rhythm grew more erratic, his mind consumed with one word: Georgiana.

She clung to his back, then she let out a delightful sigh, and he eased her onto the pillow. She smiled softly, and her eyes appeared dreamy.

Life could not entail any greater joy, and happiness shot through him. He pulled himself from her quickly, spilling seed over her taut stomach.

"That was—" Georgiana closed her eyes, as if she'd abandoned the use of words after all. Her bosom still heaved, and he stared, transfixed.

He squeezed her hand and wiped her stomach clean gently with a cloth before pulling her tightly toward him.

He'd never spent the night with a woman with whom he'd been intimate before, but now he didn't want to leave a single inch between Georgiana and him. He held her tightly, stroking her lovely, luscious locks until her head seemed to grow heavy, and her breathing grew regular.

He forced himself to stay awake, wanting to remember the exact curves of her body and angles of her face and the manner in which the candlelight flickered over it.

Only when the glow of the candlelight ran out did he allow himself to sleep, soothed by the sweet scent that still clung to her.

Chapter Twenty-six

HAPPINESS.

The emotion soared through Georgiana, undeterred by the fact she was not supposed to feel the emotion after several days traveling with the Scotsman.

She stretched, sinking blissfully in the bed, recollecting the delicious manner that Hamish's tongue and lips had claimed her.

Over and over and over again.

The bedspread remained over her, and sunbeams directed lovely warm light into the room, undaunted by the window panes. Happiness was an emotion Georgiana had felt before, but this sense of joy surpassed any emotion she might feel upon gazing at a well-composed landscape. She rolled on the bed. Staying still was a ridiculous notion, when her whole body emanated with life.

At some point Hamish had left. Perhaps he was bringing her breakfast. Georgiana had heard that men in the full throes of romance might do that. No doubt he was debating the virtues of black pudding with the innkeeper. Georgiana had always considered black pudding to be entirely without virtue, but since they were practically at the Scottish border, the innkeeper might agree with Hamish on its supposed benefits. Perhaps Georgiana might even try some today.

But no footsteps padded up the corridor to their room, and no hand pressed against the door.

She decided to dress, wrangling her shift and dress on. The action was time consuming, but when she'd made herself presentable, he still hadn't arrived.

How odd.

The happiness that had moved through her halted, replaced by an ever-stronger worry. She paced the room.

He ruined me, then left.

She pushed away the unbidden thought. It seemed too melodramatic, too similar to what other women might mourn about other men. Hamish was of course different.

Except...

She strode to the window. Though the window was not far away, she moved slowly. Trepidation filled her. Still, she opened the window and leaned her torso outside, angling her body to see—

The space where the coach should have been. A cart was in its place now, and she swallowed hard.

He'd left.

He'd really left.

Had he used her for his own masculine purposes? All women were warned of men's urges...had she simply been another casualty, ascribing emotions to him that were nonexistent?

She'd given herself freely. She'd felt womanly, desired. But now she felt foolish, a word that did not encompass either of those earlier feelings.

She combed her hair with her fingers, conscious her hands were shaking.

Maybe there was an explanation for his absence.

Memories floated through her mind. *Good* memories. Memories that made her think that the man in them couldn't possibly have abandoned her.

Had she imagined them?

But even her imagination couldn't have willed the glorious sensations that had rippled over her body the night before.

People were moving about downstairs, but he wasn't there.

The man who was always eager to leave early, determined to reach Gretna Green, had gone.

Was he heading off to Gretna Green by himself? Taking a horse to best catch up with his brother? Was he going to tell the duke to not marry into a family where one daughter had given up her maidenhood so easily?

She put on her clothes, dashed down the stairs, and exited the inn. A pleasant meadow lay before her, and she was conscious now of the sounds of a babbling brook and birds chirping. Some sheep roamed the meadow, casting occasional glances at a group of lambs who seemed to delight in leaping about.

As idyllic as the scene was, it was marred by one undeniable fact: Hamish was entirely absent from it.

She strolled farther outside and inhaled the aroma of flowers. Perhaps Hamish had decided to pick her flowers in a fit of romantic vigor.

But no dashing Scotsman appeared.

"Hamish?" she called out. "Hamish?"

The only sound she heard was birdsong, which had paused momentarily after she spoke, as if unsure whether she intended to lend her high-pitched voice to their melodies.

Uncertainty grew in her chest.

It was nonsense, she reminded herself.

Hamish wouldn't have abandoned her in some coaching inn, no matter the picturesque attractions of its location.

But he remained absent. More carriages entered and departed the inn, and the grooms shot her curious looks. She attempted to act as if it were perfectly natural for her to be outside an inn in an evening gown. Nobody came to assist her. Her dress was tattered and stained with dirt. Perhaps they assumed her to be a lady of the night. She swallowed hard, and new questions floated through her mind. Questions that related not just to why Hamish had abandoned her, but what she should possibly do now, so far from home.

I'm alone.

HAMISH URGED THE HORSES to quicken their gait. He'd been away from the inn longer than he'd desired. Georgiana might be awake by now.

Still, it had been worth it. He patted his purse and inhaled the crisp air. The sky might not be blue, but rabbits still hopped through the fields, and birds still fluttered their feathery wings. A floral scent pervaded. Spring might have come late this year, but even with fewer flowers than in past years, it most certainly had arrived.

When he rounded the final corner before the inn, he saw Georgiana at once. *Wonderful.* Her red locks flowed down, and she was gazing at the landscape. She looked every bit as lovely as she always did.

He pulled the horses over. "Climb up."

She turned toward him and widened her eyes.

He smiled. She needn't appear so shocked that they would depart now. *Or perhaps...* "Would you prefer to stay longer?"

She blinked, still silent, but then she shook her head furiously.

"I didn't think you would. Gretna Green is nearby."

If he'd realized it was so close last night, he may have had them continue on. Still, this inn was certainly more peaceful than those in its more famous neighbor village.

Georgiana strode toward the carriage, almost uncertainly. She seemed different from last night, and his heart sank. Was she regretting the passion they had shared?

She climbed onto the perch, and he smiled, conscious of her soft curves

"Is everything fine?" he asked.

"Yes," she said, but her voice sounded strained.

He hurried the horses on and soon they were on the road. "I'm sorry," he said. "I didn't want you to be worried."

"I'm fine," she said abruptly.

He assessed her, wondering if she was just acting brave.

He shook his head. Of course not. Why should she need to feign braveness? This was a pleasant day, and he'd left her in a beautiful spot.

"What were you doing?" she asked.

He hesitated, fighting the urge to share everything with her, but then shook his head. "Nothing important."

Chapter Twenty-seven

THE COACH WHEELS RUMBLED over the dirt lane. The sky had turned a deeper gray, and the wind swept over them with more force.

Georgiana resisted the urge to lean against Hamish. The warmth of his limbs may have brought comfort before, but now she focused on keeping some distance between them.

Soon they would separate...forever. She didn't need Hamish to know that fact would cause her pain.

The man hadn't offered an explanation for his absence. Had he simply wanted to take advantage of the slivers of sunlight? Could he possibly have thought the horses needed exercise? Had he felt too constrained in bed with her? Had he thought about her at all?

Hamish guided the coach into a village. Though the village resembled others they had visited, not exceeding them in beauty, many more carriages were present. Half-timbered buildings with thatched roofs lined the road. They may have lacked the majesty of their counterparts in Mayfair or Kensington, but they seemed in possession of sufficient charm. Flowers swayed in brightly painted window boxes, a rare luxury.

This was Gretna Green.

This was Scotland.

This was the end of the journey.

"What do you think?" Hamish asked.

"It's beautiful."

Hamish grinned. "I'm glad you like it."

"I do."

"But I assure you," Hamish said. "The Highlands far exceed this in beauty."

Georgiana's smile wobbled. She didn't want to think about other things. She didn't want to be reminded that Hamish's home was far away, and he was likely to want to return to it. After all, last night had been just that...one night. A single experience to remember forever.

She smoothed her tattered dress, though movement felt unnatural. Her limbs were stiff, as if already preparing for a quiet life.

There were things she could say, if she were the type of woman prone to romantic outbursts. She wanted everything for Hamish. She wanted the young boy he'd once been to be fine. The young boy who'd lost both his parents and still wanted to impress his guardians, even after they too had left this world behind. She didn't expect the man he was now to make a place for her in his life.

The man had been devastated to discover his brother's engagement. He was hardly going to desire to tie his life to the sister of the woman who would ruin his family's estate.

Young couples sat on benches beside a blacksmith's shop, and Georgiana shivered. There was something about their open affection that caused an ache to make its way through Georgiana's chest.

She didn't want to look at Hamish.

She didn't want to think about the intimate moments they'd shared. Not when soon they would have to go their separate ways.

"Don't look sad." Hamish stepped closer to her, and despite the abundances of horses on the streets, and their accompanying fragrances, Hamish's particular scent of cotton and cedar wafted over her.

For a wild, wondrous moment she thought that the man might kiss her. She gazed up, noting the way in which the sunlight shone over the chestnut strands of his hair, revealing a variety of golden colors, all of them beautiful. His eyes were filled with concern.

She stepped back rapidly, stumbling over some pebbles, and her cheeks pinkened. "I-I'm fine."

She raised her chin and squared her shoulders. *Heavens.* What was wrong with her? She didn't need him to think she was mourning the end of their time together. She wanted him to think her strong.

Perhaps she was a wallflower. Perhaps she'd just had her third season, and perhaps she'd missed her chance for love. But she would have to make do. She would find other things to keep her company. She wouldn't bemoan the fact that Hamish hadn't been born in some neighboring village in Norfolk or that he seemed far too intrigued with Lady Isla, someone to whom she could never compare. And she certainly wouldn't be anything except bright and cheerful.

He'd asked her if she was certain about the experience, and she'd said yes. It would be unfair for her to change the rules now and cling to his shirt and wish they could always remain together—something, she realized, she was regrettably tempted to do.

Gretna Green was the place for other couples to vow to spend the rest of their lives together. Not her.

She forced herself to smile and to be happy for those couples. Somewhere her sister was among them.

Of course, she didn't know just where. She glanced up, and Hamish must have seen the questioning look on her face. He certainly understood it.

"Gretna Green weddings are usually performed by anvil priests."

She blinked.

"The blacksmiths. We should go and investigate."

"Wonderful." Georgiana nodded, happy to have a plan. Now the only thing she needed to think about was how to best explain her presence to her sister and her soon-to-be brother-in-law. Hopefully the duke already was her brother-in-law, so Hamish would not feel compelled to stop the wedding.

Hamish led her toward the blacksmith's shop. He seemed to know just where everything was. The blacksmith's shop was a long, white building, and the interior was painted a similar white, though parts of it had darkened. Fires sizzled inside, and a variety of tools were perched on tables and shelves.

"It's you!" The blacksmith smiled. "But you'll need to go to the end of the line outside."

The man's friendliness was unexpected, and she blinked. "Sorry. We've come to attend a wedding."

The blacksmith looked puzzled. Evidently the weddings here did not tend to have guests.

"There are many weddings," the blacksmith's assistant said.

"Er—yes." Georgiana considered the row of couples sitting outside the man's shop. "Have you seen a blond English woman and a Scottish man? He's blond too. And—er—a duke."

The blacksmith raised his eyebrows. "I would have remembered them."

"Perhaps yesterday? Or the day before?" Georgiana's voice sounded strained, and Hamish squeezed her shoulder. She fought to resist the urge to sink into the pleasant sensation.

"They must not have arrived yet. You can wait outside."

Georgiana nodded meekly, then exited the blacksmith's shop, conscious of Hamish behind her. She scrutinized the line of couples. Some of them looked blissfully happy and excited, and others looked nervous, as if half-expecting angry relatives to ride up to put a halt to the wedding. Still others appeared resigned. None of them resembled Charlotte or the duke.

"I don't see them," Georgiana whispered. "Perhaps they're already married."

Hamish squeezed her hand.

Had she missed her sister's wedding?

Sadness moved through her.

It shouldn't be important. The ceremony would be short, scarcely a minute. The blacksmith wouldn't muse over the meaning of life and love. What did it matter if she were there to witness it?

Georgiana nodded and sank onto a bench. She was exhausted.

Where was Charlotte?

Had something horrible befallen her? Had she decided not to elope after all? Charlotte tended to have traditional urges... And if Charlotte and the duke were not coming—who would vouch for her presence? Had she destroyed her reputation for no reason at all?

"Perhaps they were married in disguise," Hamish suggested.

"They would have to use their real names for the marriage to be legal, and then—"

"—And then they would have known who they were." Hamish looked thoughtful.

He *should* have looked upset. He *should* have looked furious.

This was Georgiana's life, and now it was in tatters.

Charlotte was not here.

Georgiana's stomach churned, as if assuming she were at sea in the midst of a terrible storm, as if thinking it impossible that only her emotions tumbled against her.

She would need to resign herself to being a spinster, making the occasional cryptic comment to suggest that she had been in possession of a past—the proper sort, with occurrences in it, but to be mostly respectable and allowed to cultivate her own interests. Would she be able to ever design a garden again? She'd torn up the vicarage garden three times, and it now looked spectacular. Would she ever be able to receive a commission if her reputation was ruined? Would she be able to be taken seriously in anything if people knew she hadn't even taken her *own* reputation seriously?

It wasn't as if she could explain the rush of emotions she experienced in the presence of Hamish.

Carriages drove through the town, and she scrutinized each one for a glimpse of her sister's flaxen hair.

Most carriages when they entered Gretna Green moved slowly, as if the passengers were aware of the momentous change they were about to undergo. Though this practice was useful at allowing her to determine if her sister was present, it was always disappointing when a carriage neared them and contained strangers.

A strange heavy feeling in her stomach thickened and twisted. At some point her legs had become leaden, and if Hamish had desired her to amble, she was not certain she could have done so.

Hamish stepped forward and took her hands in his. She glanced down, conscious of the warmth that emanated from him.

Or perhaps his hands merely managed to make her heart race.

"Georgiana," he said.

Was his tone more serious than normal?

"You're wrong," he said. "There is going to be a wedding."

She blinked. "Much as you seem to take pleasure in disagreeing with me, I don't see how—"

"Then I'll tell you." He beamed, and light seemed to radiate from him.

Something seemed odd.

Hope surged within her, moving swiftly so she found herself for one ridiculous moment smiling back at him. She forced herself to halt any absurd sentimental thoughts. They'd had a pleasant few days. She'd cherish their journey forever. Every man would be compared to him, and no man would live up to him, but that was fine. At least she'd experienced time with him, and if the ache in her heart, the ache that she felt, even though she was still in his presence, even though they'd not yet separated, felt strong, that didn't mean she wanted it to go away. It would be a blissful reminder.

Perhaps Georgiana had been a bit too talkative in her seasons. Perhaps her hair had been a bit too auburn, and undecided men might perhaps have decided a bit too often to go with someone who was less likely to birth redheads who might be teased on Eton and Rugby playgrounds as being the offspring of witches. Perhaps even Georgiana had been not quite accomplished enough; her watercolors might be only tolerable. The colors she chose might be appealing in her way, but her likenesses never quite resembled her subjects enough to win praise with men whose only criterion for judging art was comparing it to reality. And though she managed to hit all the right notes in the correct order, she never managed to have that mysterious otherness that would cause people to really listen.

But despite her normalcy, she'd traveled to Scotland, all alone with Hamish. She'd experienced more of life than she could have if she'd married the first timid member of the *ton* who'd offered her to dance.

She shouldn't expect more.

Except...

Hamish kept his eyes fixed on her, and his lips were pointing in a distinctly upward direction. His eyes, always pleasant, could now be described as sparkling.

The man who'd climbed up through her balcony window and proceeded to give her insults had transformed.

A coach barreled down the street, and Hamish's lips quirked. "Those people are eager to marry."

"Y-Yes," she said, wondering what it would be like to be one of those couples, knowing that all one's betrothed wanted to do was to marry one—and hastily.

The couples' bliss seemed so far removed from anything to which she could ever aspire, and shame moved through her. For a wild moment she'd hoped for the impossible. Of course Hamish wouldn't go about proposing to her. There would be many weddings here today. That was just a fact. She shouldn't imagine things that weren't there from his attempts at conversation. Everyone knew men were less prone to good conversation than their female counterparts. It was practically a fact, and nothing that should be held against him.

The coach driver urged the horses forward. Dust rose up about them, as if seeking to mimic the clouds above.

"Whoa!" the driver called. "Whoa."

Hamish's expression immediately grew to one of concern. "It's a runaway." Hamish dashed toward it. "I'm going to help."

"Wait!" Georgiana called out, her voice wobbling, fighting nausea.

Hamish turned. "What is it?"

"It's not a runaway," she said, and her voice trembled. "I think they're just moving quickly."

"Are you certain?"

Georgiana wanted to nod, but her gaze was transfixed to the coach.

It slowed to a stop.

"You're right." Hamish's voice emanated pride, as if impressed at her cleverness.

He needn't be.

The lump in her throat grew larger.

"They don't want to marry. They're already married. The carriage—I—er—recognize it." She'd seen it many times before, and Hamish's smiling face managed to pale.

"Yoo-hoo!" A soprano voice Georgiana could never forget, would never forget soared through the village. "Georgiana!"

He swallowed hard. "It's—"

"Yes," Georgiana said.

It belonged, of course, to her mother.

Which no doubt meant that her father was also present.

Georgiana had never particularly feared her father, or, for that matter, her mother, but she suspected they might not like to discover her with Hamish.

The idea had been that she would find her sister, and her sister would vouch for her.

The idea had certainly never been that her parents would discover her, alone with an unmarried man with absolutely no chaperone in sight. Not when they would be able to discern that she'd traveled with him.

Heavens.

She hadn't meant to do this to him.

She'd sneaked onto his coach, deliberately, confident in her plan without giving him even the courtesy of discussing it with him.

If she had told him that she intended to travel alone with him all the way to Gretna Green, all the way to Scotland, he would of course have disagreed.

She hadn't given him that choice.

I have to now.

So even though Georgiana could see that it was her family's carriage, and even though she recognized her mother's voice and it seemed clear that her mother recognized her, given the enthusiasm with which her mother was shouting her name, Georgiana fled.

The action was ridiculous, but remaining was impossible. Her feet padded over the dirt lane, and she wove around the occasional puddle.

Her heartbeat quickened, as if urging her to continue faster, and she picked up her skirts and ran. Her legs burned, and her throat was dry, but it didn't matter.

All that mattered was that he not be found to have compromised her.

Chapter Twenty-eight

SHE WAS RUNNING AWAY from him.

Again.

Georgiana dashed away, as if her life depended on it.

She clutched the skirt of her dress, evidently not now bothered by the prospect of the gauze netting tearing, and rushed away, unhampered by the poor state of her slippers, or simply driven by a desire to separate from him.

And then she was gone.

This whole week they'd been together. They'd kissed, they'd been intimate, but the thought of being discovered alone with him, the thought of perhaps her parents demanding they marry... that had evidently been too much.

His heartbeat lurched, as if struggling to regain some normalcy after the vision of Georgiana rushing away from him. Perhaps he'd once known how to holler, but his throat felt dry, as if any function were now impossible.

She's gone. She's gone. She's gone.

He tightened his grasp on the ring tucked in his hand. The circular shape, with all its connotations of eternal unity, eternal bliss, mocked him.

She's gone.

His limbs were stiff, as if he were a tin soldier, some poor impression of a real man, an imperfect vision created by a

223

stranger. Perhaps his blood had simply stopped flowing into his limbs.

His heart panged. His thoughts seemed excessively sentimental, fairy tales told to children during a war when cannons were firing about around them.

He'd never been one for naivety, but where Georgiana was concerned, it seemed he'd lapsed.

He'd been so certain... So hopeful. So *happy*.

The emotion seemed ludicrous, and he cringed at the memory of riding through Gretna Green this morning. He'd been so joyous, telling every villager in sight that he needed to buy the best ring, for the very best woman. Were they peeking behind their lace curtains, laughing or saddened, depending on their particular momentary attitude toward romance?

She's gone.

The words were a refrain, one that would echo through his mind the rest of his life. At what point had she decided it would be better to flee than to marry him? Why would she choose a tarnished reputation rather than a life with him?

He should have been concerned by his brother's absence. Perhaps he'd already married Miss Charlotte Butterworth and made her his duchess. Perhaps he'd see Georgiana over holidays, and she would remain a constant reminder of the life he could have had, had he been worthy of selection.

But naturally.

He was the second son.

The spare.

He'd been convenient, no doubt easing his parents' minds and assuring them that Montgomery Castle would always be cared for. Hamish had been the emergency option if something were to befall the first choice.

If he had been expected to help look after the estate, he hadn't succeeded. Ensuring the lines in the estate's books added and subtracted in a correct fashion couldn't undo the harm Callum had done now, if he had indeed chosen to marry Miss Charlotte Butterworth.

Hamish couldn't make Georgiana a duchess. He'd have to give up the home he'd lived in. Perhaps he could continue to find architectural work, and perhaps it would be compensated better than her own father's work as a minister, but didn't Georgiana deserve everything?

He'd been in the midst of proposing to her, if in a clumsy fashion, and then she'd disappeared.

She hadn't given him a chance.

His heart twisted.

Hamish spoke in an accent that made even barmaids dismiss him, thinking him ridden with violent tendencies, perhaps because some of his ancestors had bravely defended themselves against the English invaders and had spoken of it when they arrived home.

If he married Georgiana, she would lack the large estate on which to exercise her talent for her garden design.

Hamish hadn't thought she'd considered respectability important before, but then before, she hadn't been dashing away as if her life depended on widening the distance between them.

Georgiana's parents really were approaching. The coach had stopped moving, and the groom was assisting them out.

Mrs. Butterworth had placed a gypsy bonnet over her ruffled white cap, and the veil blew in the wind. She pulled the netting down with one hand, though she'd evidently given up on securing the trimming of her bonnet, and her ribbons flayed over her, as if conspiring with the wind to make her taller and more intimidating.

She needed no help from nature to appear daunting.

"Lord Hamish!" Mrs. Butterworth shouted, unperturbed by the increased ferocity of the wind.

Hamish hesitated.

Perhaps running wasn't such a ridiculous option.

Still. He squared his shoulders and raised his chin. No doubt he deserved to be berated. He wasn't going to leave them befuddled and scrambling after him, not after they'd seen him. He owed them much more than that.

"It's really you!" Mrs. Butterworth beamed, and for a moment Hamish could see Georgiana in her mother's shining expression. She turned around. "Mr. Butterworth! I told you it was the duke's brother, and it is. How good I am at spotting people."

Mr. Butterworth ducked his head from the coach. Perhaps Mrs. Butterworth was experiencing a momentary delight at recognizing someone hundreds of miles away from where she'd last seen him, but Mr. Butterworth appeared less contemplative about the wonders of that fact. His eyebrows shot together, and his demeanor exuded anger.

When he'd first met Mr. Butterworth, the man had been comfortably ensconced in an armchair, taking such delight in the comforts of well-crafted upholstery and pillows, even the silky ones that some men preferred to eschew, that Hamish had imagined that the man might avoid discomfort.

Instead, Mr. Butterworth had not only traveled to Gretna Green, he was now barreling from the coach, with the vigor of a well-lit cannonball, and was heading toward Hamish. Mud spattered about the man's buckskin breeches, but his pace did not diminish. He wrestled Hamish to the ground and settled each thigh on either side of him.

Clearly Mr. Butterworth did not subscribe to the *ton*'s tenements for propriety.

"You do not mess with a Norfolk man," Mr. Butterworth said.

"You're a v-vicar," Hamish stammered.

"And you're heading for hell." Mr. Butterworth sneered. His teeth were set into a ferocious line, and he directed both fists at Hamish. He pressed against Hamish, as if to thrust him faster into hell that way.

Birds fluttered merrily above Hamish, evidently unconcerned at his downfall

"Must you be so dramatic?" Mrs. Butterworth asked. "The dear man will think you're a Methodist."

Hamish blinked.

"We're not Methodists," Mrs. Butterworth said in a voice obviously meant to be reassuring, though she made no move to assist her husband from his newfound perch on top of Hamish's body.

"The denomination you subscribe to is of no concern," Hamish said.

This time even Mrs. Butterworth gasped. Hamish had the distinct feeling he'd said the wrong thing. The wind continued to bluster, slamming against him, as if deciding to thrash him even if Mr. Butterworth had decided to postpone his pummeling.

"Where is my daughter?" Mr. Butterworth bellowed, shifting his position, as if rallying each serving he'd ever eaten, each mince pie, each marzipan delicacy, each marmalade tartlet, to harm Hamish.

Hamish hesitated.

Georgiana wouldn't want him to admit her location.

"She's—er—not here," Hamish lied.

Mr. Butterworth's face darkened. "Just because I have *pince-nez* and cannot see with them off, does not mean I can't see with them on. I saw my daughter. She was just speaking with you. And then she ran away. Where is she?"

"I—" Hamish swallowed hard. "I'm sorry. I—I couldn't say where she is."

"She ran away, darling," Mrs. Butterworth explained, as if that could possibly explain anything. "Perhaps she was desirous of exercise."

"Yes," Hamish nodded eagerly.

"That's nonsense," Mr. Butterworth said. "My daughter is a civilized woman, not given to fits of spontaneous running."

"Habits can always be formed, my dear." Mrs. Butterworth's voice was soothing, like the mother he'd wished he'd had, like the mother he would never have.

"She is obviously running away from this man." Mr. Butterworth pointed a finger at Hamish, and he shrank back. "You stole our daughter."

Stealing wasn't the right word.

Hamish hadn't kidnapped her.

He hadn't known she was in his coach.

But Mr. Butterworth needed someone to dislike now, and Hamish could be that person.

Hamish looked around, wondering if Mr. Butterworth intended to drag him into the blacksmith's shop and have the blacksmith thrust fiery things in his face until Mr. Butterworth had managed to wrangle his daughter to return so they might marry.

I would be happy to do so.

But Mr. Butterworth did no such thing.

"You're going to listen to me," Mr. Butterworth said, articulating each word expertly, despite the wind and stomp of horses' hooves about them. "You are going to return to the Highlands, up onto your craggy peak, with only goats and ruins to keep you company, and you are never going to mention to anyone that you traveled alone with my daughter."

"You're not going to make them marry?" Mrs. Butterworth's voice was mournful. "This is the ideal spot to do so. And elopements are so *en vogue* now. She will be quite fashionable when she returns to society."

"As I said in the coach," Mr. Butterworth huffed, and Hamish had the impression that they'd had this conversation many times before, "I am not forcing my daughter to wed anyone. I, for one, have read Mary Wollstonecraft and I refuse to subjugate my daughter to anything dreadful."

"But marriage!" Mrs. Butterworth wailed. "How could that be considered dreadful?"

Mr. Butterworth refrained from reconsidering the merits of marriage. "Georgiana fled. She obviously considers this man to be no friend, much less her perpetual mate."

The words should not have been particularly brutal. They contained not a single curse, and he knew he should be grateful that Mr. Butterworth made no demand for a marriage. Many members of the *ton* would have desired that their fathers-in-law shared his characteristics. And yet, Hamish's only emotion was grief.

He struggled from Mr. Butterworth's clasp. "I'll—er—go to the inn across the road. If you need me, well, I'll be there."

And he left.

Hamish had been injured in the war before, and had found the experience to be excruciating and best forgotten, even though his body had healed, unlike the new Duke of Alfriston's leg. Still, the sudden pain that jolted through his body seemed entirely comparable. But unlike when a bullet had entered his right arm and another piece of shrapnel had entered his left arm, he knew that he could not simply wait for the surgeon and time to do their work.

His heart wouldn't stop aching, no matter how often medical experts examined it.

Because Georgiana had run away from him.

He removed his purse and took out the ring he'd picked up in Gretna Green earlier that day. The perfect sapphire stone set on the shimmering silver band seemed foolish, and he tucked it back into his purse.

He'd been trying to propose to Georgiana, but it seemed like she'd given him her answer.

He strode rapidly away from Georgiana's parents. He'd imagined, evidently with great foolishness that they might become *his* parents.

They were warm and kindhearted. *Well.* Neither word seemed to describe their current behavior toward him, but that was easily ascribed to the fact that they were also fiercely protective of Georgiana.

Would his own parents have been as protective toward him, if they had lived? He already knew that they had been neither warm nor kindhearted, though perhaps that had more to do with him than with them. Perhaps if he'd been different, his early memories of his time at Montgomery Castle would not be confined to the nursery and his nursemaids.

After all, the only people who had shown him affection—Lord and Lady McIntyre—had been wrong to do so. Even though he had known how important it was for them that the Montgomery and McIntyre family might be officially joined together, he hadn't been able to convince his very own brother to fulfill the vow. What use was he?

He wanted his brother to be happy and not regret a life he'd happened upon through rash impulsivity. Perhaps Callum had found happiness. Hamish had been foolish to dream that he could find the same happiness.

He ambled through the village, passing low half-timbered homes with heavy thatched roofs. When he'd visited this morning he'd been full of hope, imagining ridiculous thoughts for the future. He'd pondered whether Georgiana might enjoy decorating their home, so that her parents might have a place to stay should they decide to visit for long periods of time.

They wouldn't visit.

They didn't even desire his help now.

And she's gone.

Chapter Twenty-nine

GEORGIANA RUSHED THROUGH Gretna Green. Happy couples, their hands linked in bliss, stared at her with bewilderment. Their lower lips dropped down, and their eyes widened, as if the mere vision of Georgiana was a cause for facial exercise. But then she must appear ridiculous.

Long tears impaled the netting of her gown, once so carefully adorned with ribbons and flounces. No doubt she appeared like some nightmarish bride. This had once been her best dress, but only a few short days had rendered it destroyed.

Just like my dreams.

"Where's your husband?" a villager called out.

"She's 'aving doubts," a woman shouted, and Georgiana's face heated.

She wasn't having doubts.

She had no husband.

No betrothed.

And now I never will.

Her parents were here, and now they knew she was ruined. At some point, she'd feel humiliation and distress, but now her thoughts remained with Hamish. She'd succumbed to the man's charms, finding the man in ample possession of them, even though her first impression of him had been negative.

Tears stung and prickled her eyes, rendering her blind to everything except the recent occurrence.

Last night—earlier than that, she'd allowed herself to imagine a life with Hamish. She should have relegated it to a schoolgirl fantasy. She'd told herself that last night hadn't mattered, that it had been driven by curiosity, but the notion was ridiculous.

Last night hadn't meant something because she had gained more knowledge of the world than before. For that she had only to pick up one of her father's many tomes, the sort that he was always recommending. No, last night had meant something purely because of Hamish.

It hadn't been about knowledge or the satisfaction of any scientific puzzlement that occurred when reading certain penny dreadfuls.

It had been about Hamish.

Hamish's hands brushing against hers. Hamish's lips on hers. Hamish's eyes on her. And then...Hamish inside her, and the strange ripple of emotion, of sheer physical pleasure, that had accompanied it.

They'd slept in each other's arms last night. She'd wondered at how his body had felt so right pressed against hers, how their figures, their heights, had seemed to meld into an easy perfection.

Last night had been a fantasy.

She'd known it when he hadn't appeared beside her this morning.

She'd known it when he'd abandoned her.

And she'd even known it when he'd reappeared, making conversation about nothing important, and showing no sign in the least that he was distressed they would never see each other again.

The wind whirled about her, lifting up her locks in a manner any illustrator at *Matchmaking for Wallflowers* might eagerly depict to her detriment. The wind threatened to swoop up the hem of her dress, and she shivered, placing her hands tightly about her.

She was cold and wet. Her slippers had been destroyed ever since that first night in which she'd wandered into the woods. Water seeped into the thin soles. A sealskin coat would be useful now, but she didn't even have a spencer. She was dressed for a wedding, not for a cold afternoon in northern Britain.

She hadn't found her sister, wasn't assured that at least she was going to marry the man of her dreams. Nothing had been accomplished.

And now she would have to join her parents and listen to how she'd destroyed their dreams for her.

She paused. The tension that had ricocheted through her, ceased.

All that was left was sorrow.

Her eyes stung more, and then her cheeks dampened, and then even her breath seemed difficult to control. She swallowed and gasped, sputtered and gulped.

She sobbed.

The sound was horrid.

Weeds, damp from rain and not some idyllic dew, clung to her dress.

This was Scotland, but it was Scotland without the views of lochs, without the isles, without the mountains. The land was flat, and the mocking laughs of the villagers still echoed in her ears.

"Georgiana," a baritone voice said.

She tensed, recognizing the sound.

It was her father.

She rubbed her face, attempting to feign some semblance of dignity, but there was none to be had. Tears smeared her face. No doubt her skin was red and blotchy, as if seeking to match her hair.

She blinked hard, willing herself to have misheard, but footsteps padded behind her.

"Now carrying handkerchiefs may require a foresight for unhappiness that I am unwilling to plan for, but I find that my cravat can be quite multifunctional."

"Papa?" She turned her head toward him, and he unwound his cravat and handed it to her. "You must use it. Goodness knows I'll never figure out how to put it on without a mirror."

She smiled, despite everything, and he returned it.

He wasn't angry.

"This is not what a cravat is supposed to be used for," she said.

"If it can help my little girl one tiny bit, then it's the very best use for it."

She smiled again, blinking away her tears. She dabbed her face with the linen. "You must think me so foolish."

"I never could," he said solemnly. "Your mother told me you'd gone to stop him."

"I thought she might—"

"But it took me getting her two servings of lemon ice before she told. That's a record for her."

She giggled softly, though it wasn't exactly pleasure that she felt.

"She was worried about you," Papa said, his voice gentle. "You know that's why she told."

Georgiana nodded.

"I just wish we could have arrived sooner," he said.

"I should have known better," she said softly, her heart aching. "I knew better. Everyone says to stay away from—"

"Roguish men?"

She nodded, and the tears flooded. "I just thought, for Charlotte's sake..."

"That was brave of you," he said. "The reason everyone warns about it is that emotions can seem impossible to control. You're not the first person to succumb to a scoundrel, and you won't be the last."

"Why are you so nice? I was impetuous and impulsive and—"

"Don't you wonder how I married your mother?" Papa asked. "A man like me, no matter how stuffy and scholarly you might find me, is not supposed to have anything to do with the niece of an earl."

She smiled.

"Your mother took a chance on me, and you took a chance on Lord Hamish. It's unfortunate that he didn't live up to that chance—and I very nearly strangled him—"

"You didn't, Papa!" Georgiana felt her eyes widen, and her lower lip dropped downward.

He nodded. "I was the cricket champion for five years running of our green. I can wield more than a cricket bat."

Despite everything, she laughed.

He patted her back. "There, there, my dear."

She sniffed and dabbed the tears from her face. A rain shower wouldn't be entirely unwanted now. She dreaded walking into the village again.

"I've always thought it curious why Beau Brummel goes about recommending cravats to everyone, but after reading about his gambling losses, I understand," Papa said.

"That's not why he recommends them." Georgiana smiled through her sobs. Her chest still felt hollow, her heart still ached, and goodness her breath remained uneven, but at least she still had her family.

Chapter Thirty

HAMISH PACED THE BEDROOM of the posting house. The slanted floorboards creaked and groaned beneath him, as if to provide a melody to his despair.

The sky remained a less eager participant for gloom. It had long ceased raining. Hamish had always adored the long summer days in Scotland, but now he cursed the bright light that continued to illuminate the blacksmiths' shops and its streams of joyous couples.

His heart ached. Pain surged through his body, but there was no French uniformed soldier whom he could vanquish. Only Georgiana could heal his sorrow, and she'd made it clear that she abhorred his presence. Perhaps she regretted their night together, regretted everything—

After all, she'd fled.

He'd spotted her with her parents. She was being cared for, and Hamish would never mention to anyone that he'd traveled to Gretna Green with her. Perhaps her parents would manage to keep her reputation intact, and she might marry. Perhaps in time this trip would be little more than a memory of a nightmare: something to expend with as much efficiency as she'd expended Hamish.

To think he'd suggested Callum not marry Charlotte. Hamish knew now that love knew no logic, and yet a failure to adhere to it only brought agony. No wonder Callum had not taken Hamish's warnings with any seriousness.

And where *was* Callum?

Hamish had been so certain he'd find them in Gretna Green. He pushed away images of carriage accidents from his mind. He didn't want to contemplate that. Besides... If a couple had gotten seriously harmed, whether by a carriage accident or by highwaymen, surely someone at one of the many posting inns he'd visited would have mentioned it.

No.

His unhappiness did not derive from concerns over his brother's safety, but from the fact he did not want to spend the rest of his life without Georgiana.

He sat on the immense four-poster bed piled high with feather mattresses. The room was more elegant than any of the other posting houses. The decor must have agreed with other guests, given the sounds of vigorous pleasure taking drifting through the walls.

Hamish gritted his teeth, but his mind returned to Georgiana.

Perhaps it always would.

She'd been odd this morning

Aloof.

I shouldn't have left her.

He fingered the ring in his pocket. He'd thought it beneficial to make the proposal special to her. Perhaps most people didn't propose with rings, and perhaps it was a continental tradition, and Britain had just battled the French—but Georgiana was special, and he wanted her to know.

It had seemed appropriate to pop into the neighboring town to get a ring. He'd wanted to start their marriage correctly. He'd wanted her to know that he took her seriously. The Scottish borders was a wonderful place to procure such an item, given the influx of romantic minded people here with sufficient wealth to make the inconvenient journey and pay for the blacksmith's hefty fees to save a few days inconvenience of waiting for the banns to be published.

He'd been intimate with her, and she'd been a maiden.

God in heaven. Perhaps she hadn't realized he'd been attempting to propose to her. She needed to know he loved her. He needed to tell her.

Even if she might say that she didn't return his affection. Even if she said no to his proposal.

Even if he might make a fool of himself.

Perhaps she thought that he wouldn't desire to marry her, but she was wrong.

Hamish was not going to tarry a moment more.

He needed to clutch her in his arms, and he needed to tell her that he adored her.

That he loved her.

That he'd thought her beautiful and fascinating when he first saw her, but that now he couldn't imagine a life without her. If there was the slightest chance that she returned his affections—and he thought there might just be—well, he was going to do his best to let her know.

He grabbed his cloak and swung it around his shoulders. She wasn't staying in this inn—he'd watched from the window—there was only one other inn in which she might be. The family wouldn't want to leave Gretna Green when there was a chance Callum and Charlotte would appear.

Hamish rushed down the stairs, past the startled innkeeper and dashed into the street. His feet slid against this afternoon's mud, splattering onto his Hessians. People directed their gazes at him, as if scrutinizing him was more interesting than telling their new spouse about the exact extent of their affection.

It didn't matter.

All that mattered in this whole world was Georgiana.

He loved her. He adored her. He wanted to marry her.

And he wanted to spend a very long, very full life with her.

She was the love of his life, and he needed her to know how much he cared. He didn't want to put her through a night of misery, thinking he'd let her go easily. He squared his shoulders. If she didn't return his love, she could tell him.

He arrived at the other posting house. Lights glowed from some of the windows, and he stood, trying to make out if she was inside. His boots sank into the mud, and horses and carriages rumbled by him.

His heart danced in his chest. For a wild moment, he considered bursting into song like the hero in some Italian opera who showed up late in the third act after having broken out of a prison from which he was falsely being held.

Since disturbing the wedding nights of happy couples might cause him to be dragged away, he refrained from singing.

Instead, he waited, hoping he would see her at one of the windows. The minutes seemed long, but finally, he saw her. He'd memorized her silhouette and the exact manner in which she ran her fingers through her hair when she was nervous.

Hamish inhaled and looked around for a helpful tree or balcony.

This posting inn did not seem to be in possession of either. It might, though, be in possession of a ladder, and Hamish walked around the perimeter. Unfortunately, the inn was immaculately maintained, a fact that probably brought pleasure to the guests, but was not immediately helpful.

The blacksmith's shop.

They would have a ladder.

Hamish sprinted to it, pounding his feet over the dirt road. He shouted a greeting and a quick explanation to the startled blacksmiths, grabbed the ladder, then hauled it onto his shoulder. The exercise was more difficult than he'd assumed, and he felt a sudden burst of warmth for all the people who'd managed to construct buildings taller than a single story. He'd never quite comprehended the difficulty that it entailed.

Once Hamish had secured the ladder on his shoulder he marched to the inn, ignoring the slight wobble from the unwieldy load. More people seemed to be scrutinizing him, this time pointing him to the others. *Never mind.* Shyness could be for another time.

Hamish rested the ladder against the window and looked around. Thankfully, the innkeeper had not noticed him, and he scrambled up the rickety steps. He pushed against the window and—

Nothing happened.

Evidently Georgiana had thought to lock it.

Despite Hamish's appreciation for the increased interest she was taking in her safety, he would have preferred to enter the room. His plan had not involved standing on a ladder and trying to get her attention through a closed window. He tapped against the glass pane.

And tapped again.

And tapped again.

"It's a ghost!" A scream came from the room, and Hamish's heart sank.

It was not Georgiana's voice—it was her mother's.

Had he gone to the wrong room? Murmurings sounded, and the window was pulled open. He stared straight into Georgiana's angry, defiant eyes. Declarations of love were evidently not her primary instinct upon seeing him. Behind Georgiana was her mother, and behind *her* was Georgiana's father.

Hamish's heart thudded in earnest.

"It's no ghost. It's the duke's blasted brother," Mr. Butterworth growled, evidently viewing Hamish's presence as sufficiently catastrophic so as to curse.

"Naturally," Mrs. Butterworth said, adjusting her cap. "I recognized him myself."

Hamish was glad his presence brought Georgiana's mother some pride. He squared his shoulders and willed his voice not to quiver. "Aye."

"That lovely accent," Mrs. Butterworth exclaimed "Every word sounds so musical. Tell me, are you musical?"

"He'll soon be without a larynx." Mr. Butterworth rushed toward him. For the son of a vicar, and a vicar himself, and a man known to adore even the more tiresome appearing books, Mr. Butterworth was remarkably athletic. Even in the dim light, Hamish could see the bulge of the man's muscle, visible through his thin nightshirt, and the man's running pace was definitely of the quick variety. Evidently, taking long walks while writing his sermons was beneficial for his health as well as for its inspirational purposes.

Hamish clasped his fingers more tightly around the ladder.

"Papa!" Georgiana said. "You mustn't hurt him."

"You always do preach that murder is a sin," Mrs. Butterworth added, and Hamish waited as Georgiana's father considered this statement.

"Is there a reason why you are here?" Mr. Butterworth asked, his voice still filled with suspicion, even if the rest of the man's body no longer seemed intent on dismembering him.

For now.

"I would like to speak with Georgiana," Hamish said.

"Miss Butterworth to you," her father said.

"I would like to make her Lady Hamish Montgomery."

Georgiana's eyes widened, and her face was inscrutable. Hamish cursed the dim light. But shouldn't she be saying something, anything?

"There will be a wedding," Hamish continued. "That's what I was trying to tell you, Georgiana. Before you ran off. *Our* wedding."

"We—"

"Will marry," he said. "If, of course, you'll have me."

"But—" Georgiana paused, as if she couldn't be certain that she'd heard correctly. He hoped she'd not chosen to be silent because she was trying to think of a way to reject his proposal.

Perhaps she'd understood him before when he'd started to propose. Perhaps she was flummoxed he hadn't been able to discern her lack of interest in him when she'd run away.

"Why?" she asked finally.

It was not the squeal of pleasure he would have preferred, but at least she was listening.

"Not because of duty," he said, hoping to assure her.

"Well, that's no surprise," Mr. Butterworth grumbled. "The man most blatantly lacks it."

"It's because I adore you," Hamish said quickly. "Because I love you. Because I can't imagine a world where you are not part of it, and because I don't want to try."

"How romantic!" Mrs. Butterworth sighed and clasped her hands together.

"He's not proposing to you," Mr. Butterworth said.

"But he is doing it in front of me," Mrs. Butterworth said. "That is somewhat similar."

"Vaguely similar," Mr. Butterworth conceded.

Georgiana remained quiet.

God in heaven. Hamish wanted to hear from her, no matter how helpful it was for his self-esteem to learn Mrs. Butterworth found the proposal contained romantic appeal.

"Georgiana?" Hamish's voice sounded hoarse, as if he'd been waiting for her answer for so long that all the water in his mouth had dried, like some abandoned potted plant. "What do you say?"

"I don't know," she said.

"I want to marry you."

"But—"

"I love you." He smiled. "If you didn't notice already."

"So it's not to protect my reputation?" she asked. "Because it's quite kind of you to be gentlemanly, but I wouldn't want you to feel compelled to marry me because I hid in your coach."

"Georgiana!" her mother exclaimed. "Have you learned nothing during your three seasons?"

Mr. Butterworth put a hand on his wife's shoulder. "This is our daughter's decision. Not yours." He directed a glance at Georgiana. "And just say the word, my dear, and I will topple him off that ladder."

"You two are impossible." Mrs. Butterworth huffed, and though Hamish could not tell in the dim light whether she was rolling her eyes, he rather thought she might be.

"Georgiana," Hamish said. "I am not proposing because I feel compelled to protect your reputation. Do you think that a man who climbed into your room would be so driven by society's rules?"

"Perhaps not."

"And if I had adopted a guilty conscience I could always set you up in a nice cottage just like I'd planned for your sister. The money is still there." His face grew sober.

"You can't be serious," she said.

"I am. Your happiness is the only thing of importance. Though I rather hope you will want to find happiness with me."

His chest tightened. She seemed contemplative, and worry ricocheted through him. He clasped her hands, clutching her slender fingers, and hoping he would never have to let go. "Do you care for me?"

He sucked in the cold night air, but the action could not keep his heartbeat from continuing to quicken, because the prospect of her *not* desiring to marry him was terrible. "Because I love you. I adore you. You're brave and smart and kind and lovely."

She was silent.

God in heaven.

This was not going well. His heart squeezed, and he resisted the temptation to slink back to the other inn. "I know we haven't known each other that long, and if you prefer to return to London, I would be happy to court you, should you give me permission."

She remained silent, though her night rail rustled, and she seemed to have narrowed the distance between them.

Did she not even want him to court her? His heart pounded fiercely, as if it had turned into some wild animal, captured and forced away from his mate, who would never be able to return.

"I don't think seeing you during afternoon calls will be suitable for me," Georgiana said, and Hamish's heart broke.

"I don't think I would be able to go through with it," she continued, still clutching his hands.

"Are you certain, Georgiana dear?" her mother asked.

Mr. Butterworth stepped forward. "I think you should descend that ladder immediately, young man."

Georgiana held up her hand to stop her father, and Hamish wondered whether she would proceed to catalog all the ways he'd harmed her.

He deserved them.

He deserved anything she would say.

"I cannot accept your offer to court me," Georgiana said, "Because I would like to accept your offer to marry me."

This time Hamish was silent.

Had she just said that?

Had he conjured up the most delicious words in the world?

"I accept your offer," Georgiana said, and her voice sounded warm. "I'll marry you."

Hamish's heart sang. It crescendoed. It soared. If there had been indeed a wild animal trapped in his chest, it was now safely returned to its beloved.

Chapter Thirty-one

HAMISH WAS STANDING before her and saying the most wonderful things.

Jubilation filled the room.

Her mother squealed and clapped her hands.

"I want you," Georgiana breathed. "I want you forever and always."

His eyes sparkled, and a thrill shot through Georgiana that she had given him such pleasure.

"Then marry me. Now."

Hamish grabbed Georgiana's hand, and she pulled him into her bedroom. She slid on her mother's pelisses, and they then dashed through the inn and toward the blacksmith's shop. Her parents followed them. They strode together through Gretna Green, and if Hamish had pointed out that they were floating, she wouldn't have been surprised.

The other couples were gone. Evidently they'd already been married, and Hamish and Georgiana entered the blacksmith's shop.

"What is it now?" The blacksmith looked up. "I told you I haven't seen them. I would recall another Scotsman with a blond Englishwoman."

"There's going to be a wedding," Hamish announced.

The blacksmith raised his eyebrows. "There is always going to be a wedding. People are always getting married. They've no idea of how thoroughly pedestrian they are being."

"But this is different," Hamish declared. "This time I am getting married."

"Oh." The blacksmith set aside his tools and brushed sooty hands over his apron. "I suppose you'll be wanting to marry immediately."

Hamish nodded. "I don't want to tarry a second."

"Isn't it romantic?" Mrs. Butterworth's voice soared through the blacksmith's shop, as if she were testing whether she might break the iron with the same efficiency a soprano might shatter glass.

The iron pieces the blacksmith had made remained resolutely in place, unfazed by Mrs. Butterworth's exuberance. The latter had moved from hollering to balancing a covered basket on a table filled with all manner of iron objects.

The blacksmith's face managed to pale, and he moved quickly toward the basket and placed it on the ground.

"There will be a wedding," the blacksmith, in a tone that indicated that he'd long stopped seeing weddings as anything except an interlude for when his irons needed to cool.

"Indeed! And we must prepare!" Mrs. Butterworth bent down and fiddled with the basket. In the next moment, she was scattering flowers and herbs about the establishment. "This is for happiness, this is for health, and this is for wealth!"

"I'm sorry," Georgiana mouthed, but Hamish only smiled.

HAMISH'S MOTHER HAD died, but Mrs. Butterworth seemed to have the energy for two mothers. There just might be something nice about becoming part of a noisy, close-knit family.

The blacksmith's face furrowed. "Those are flowers."

"And dried herbs," Mr. Butterworth said. "Herbs have quite a good many purposes."

"And none of them belong in my blacksmith's shop." The blacksmith's teeth were definitely clenched now, and Hamish wondered whether that was because he suspected Mrs. Butterworth's eccentricity could only be the result of a privileged background, the sort that might involve generous tips.

"Why don't we do the wedding outside?" the blacksmith suggested.

"Oh." Mrs. Butterworth appeared puzzled.

"That will be romantic as well," Georgiana assured her. "Now, let's go."

They stepped outside into the cool Scottish wind. The breeze rustled the flowers on the trees, and a crowd of people outside gathered around them perhaps seeing it as a good practice session for their own wedding services.

The blacksmith took Hamish's and Georgiana's names, managing to not grumble about the late hour.

"Montgomery," the assistant blacksmith said. "I have a letter for you."

Hamish halted his embrace. "A letter?"

The man nodded and shuffled through some papers, then held it up triumphantly. "It just arrived."

Hamish took the letter, recognizing his brother's handwriting. His hands trembled, unsure what he would find.

Though he'd longed for his brother to break off the engagement to secure Montgomery Castle, it now seemed every bit as vital that he marry her. Hamish was part of the Butterworth family now and he did not want anything to harm it.

He tore the letter open, noting that it didn't have the normal ducal seal. Callum must have written it hastily.

"Read it aloud," Georgiana said.

He nodded.

Whatever the contents were, Charlotte's parents deserved to know.

"My dear brother,

If you are reading this, then you must be in Gretna Green. Enjoy your beloved Scotland and don't become too bored, because I will not be there to entertain you."

"He's not marrying her," Mr. Butterworth said, and Hamish despised the man's mournful tone.

"You mustn't be so melodramatic," Mrs. Butterworth said, chiding her husband. "Do continue, dear."

"Charlotte and I will marry in Guernsey," Hamish read.

Georgiana clapped her hands. "The Channel Islands! I-I feel so foolish. I never imagined she would go anywhere else except Gretna Green."

He kissed her head. "I am very glad you thought they were going here."

She smiled, and for a moment it seemed impossible to do anything else except stare at her.

He forced his gaze away. "And there's a note from your sister."

"Read it," Mr. Butterworth said.

"I am happy and well," Charlotte had written.

"Well, of course, she's happy and well," Mrs. Butterworth said. "She's marrying a duke."

"But eloping...Going on a ship..." Georgiana shook her head. "She's never been on water before."

"Then perhaps it is time," Mrs. Butterworth said. "They're happy. That's what is important."

Georgiana beamed and squeezed Hamish's hand. "They're happy."

He gazed at her, wondering again at her bravery, wondering at how fortunate it was that she'd climbed into his coach, and not imagining a world without her.

He gazed down at the ring on her hand and realized he did not have to.

Hamish inhaled the air.

He should feel cold, but warmth coursed through his body. Soon he would be married to Georgiana, the most wonderful woman in the world.

Epilogue

SCOTLAND
   1822

The trees had turned golden and garnet, as if dipped into paint by some particularly enthusiastic child, and Hamish lay on a blanket in the meadow. The grass was a dark deep green, the result of months of rain, but now the vibrant shade was exquisite, richer than even the finest emerald.

Hamish dipped his quill into ink and wrote a few more phrases.

Footsteps padded toward him, and the hem of a navy dress met his eyes.

He smiled. He knew that hem. He'd done pleasant things underneath its flounces, and he tilted up his head, recognizing the delightful curves of his wife's form, her wide smile, and ever sparkling eyes.

"Darling." Georgiana leaned down and kissed him, and he was shrouded in her delightful auburn locks and lost in her impossibly sweet scent. "How is the design coming along?"

"Splendid," Hamish murmured.

His wife settled onto the blanket.

The sunlight was in full force today, and she shaded her eyes with her hand. He followed her gaze to their manor home.

It wasn't the same place he had once shared with Callum. It was his very own home. It wasn't a castle, and had never been used in a defensive manner, but he adored it.

Tourelles perched on rounded towers, and stepped gables adorned the roof in a manner suited for the German fairytales his daughters had taken to reading. The rose-hued sandstone differed from the somber gray stone he'd been accustomed to that had seemed to desire to meld into the oft-stormy clouds.

Georgiana had insisted on a home that was not set on a craggy clifftop, no matter how many romantic painters from Germanic lands might come to paint it. Though he'd teased her that she was recreating Norfolk, they had found the perfect property, and it was reassuring to know that his daughters were less likely to be tossed into the sea if the North Wind decided to send out strong gales.

"I love you," he said.

"I love you too." Georgiana squeezed his hand. "And to think, none of this would have happened if we hadn't gone to Gretna Green."

Hamish pulled her closer to him, no matter how scandalous they might appear to servants. Musing about a world which may not have contained Georgiana brought him no joy.

"I'm glad we gave the blacksmith some work to do," Hamish said.

"Mama did scatter a lot of flowers."

"I know now why flower girls are always under the age of five. Smaller arms."

Georgiana laughed. "I did actually come to fetch you."

"Not to muse about our wedding?"

She shook her head. "The ball is in a few hours, and I want you to see the decorations."

"I'm sure they're perfect."

"Well, that is a given."

Hamish stood up and picked up his papers, thrusting them against his chest while he grabbed the blanket with his other hand.

"I can help—" Georgiana started to say, but Hamish shook his head and headed to the estate house. Georgiana strode beside him.

Music wafted from an open window. The music was jovial and did not resemble the somber gentleness present at Almack's that had rendered every country music song staid.

They entered their home.

"See that these go in the library." Hamish handed the butler his materials.

"Certainly." The butler tilted his torso in a downward direction while tightening the cap of the ink. He soon disappeared around the corner.

Hamish took Georgiana's hand in his, not minding the rough feel of her lace gloves in the slightest. Perhaps people of their class refrained from showing open affection, though Hamish suspected this restraint stemmed more from unhappy marriages than virtue, but Hamish was not most men. Blast it, Georgiana was his wife and the presence of two delightful daughters in the manor house should prepare the servants for the realization that their relationship involved touching.

Hamish and Georgiana strode up the wooden steps to the ballroom. Paintings of the Highlands and Isle of Skye adorned the walls. The sober portraits of past ancestors could remain at

Montgomery Castle: Hamish refused to feel driven by duty to solely serve them any longer.

The music was stronger on this floor, and he opened the door of the ballroom.

"Papa!" Footsteps rushed toward him, and first one daughter, then the other appeared. Hamish knelt, and they catapulted toward him, as if in training to be cricket balls in the hands of an expert player.

"I couldn't keep them from dancing," their nursemaid said.

"Dancing is good." He grinned. "Can you show me?"

The girls squealed and clapped their hands.

"You should join them," Georgiana said.

"As should you, my dear."

They danced together, leaping to the sounds of a Scottish reel.

In the summer, when the roads were at their smoothest, they would make the journey to Norfolk to visit Georgiana's relatives. Isolation was no longer something he believed in, and perhaps when Marianne and Lily were older, they might venture across the channel. His daughters would grow up to be curious.

"Don't forget to admire the banquet table," Georgiana said.

"I hope admiring involves tasting." He sauntered toward the long table. Scotch eggs and haggis perched on blue and white china as if they were French delicacies, and he inhaled the rich scent of wild game beside them. Vibrant-colored punch lay in crystal tumblers, and fruit floated inside.

"It's perfect," he said. "As are you."

Georgiana's cheeks pinkened, but she smiled. "Your valet will want you to change into your evening clothes now."

"I can be tardy. Let's ask the musicians to play a waltz."

"But it's not Scottish."

"I don't care."

He led Georgiana back to the dance section of the ballroom and murmured instructions to the musicians.

Soon the joyful strains of a waltz played, and he twirled and swirled his wife about the dancefloor as happiness jolted through him.

About the Author

BORN IN TEXAS, BIANCA Blythe spent four years in England. She worked in a fifteenth-century castle, though sadly that didn't actually involve spotting dukes and earls strutting about in Hessians.

She credits British weather for forcing her into a library, where she discovered her first Julia Quinn novel. Thank goodness for blustery downpours.

Bianca now lives in California with her husband.

WEDDING TROUBLE

MATCHMAKING FOR WALLFLOWERS

Mad About the Baron
A Marquess for Convenience
The Wrong Heiress for Christmas

THE SLEUTHING STARLET
Murder at the Manor House
Danger on the Downs
The Body in Bloomsbury
A Continental Murder

Printed in Great Britain
by Amazon

43766478R00148